D1071589

FRANK NORRIS

OF "THE WAVE" & *Stories
& Sketches from the San Francisco
weekly,* 1893 *to* 1897. *Foreword
by Charles G. Norris. Introduction by
Oscar Lewis.*

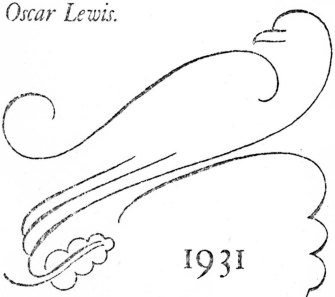

1931

San Francisco :: The Westgate Press

Republished 1972
Scholarly Press, Inc., 22929 Industrial Drive East
St. Clair Shores, Michigan 48080

Library of Congress Cataloging in Publication Data

orris, Frank, 1870-1902.
    Frank Norris of "The Wave."

    CONTENTS: Bandy Callaghan's girl.--His sister.--End
of the beginning. [etc.]
    I. Title.
PS2471.N6 1972   813'.4   78-131789
ISBN 0-403-00676-7

76-284

FOREWORD

by

CHARLES G. NORRIS

THE *collection of the material in this book and its publication give me much satisfaction. It represents my brother's work during his most formative years. He was finding himself during this time—from early '96 to late '98—with more certainty of purpose than at any other period of his life. With the single exception of Professor Gates of Harvard, under whom he took one year of postgraduate work after leaving the University of California, he received little encouragement from anyone. Possibly my mother believed*

he had talent, but his work was too brutal and too realistic for her poetical and mid-Victorian mind. I remember immediately after "The Jongleur of Taillebois" was published in The Wave, *a friend of my father's met him on Montgomery Street and said: "If I had a son who wrote a story like that, I'd have put him out of the world in a lethal chamber." If this was not the exact method of annihilating Frank, at least it was to have been complete. My father was greatly disturbed, and never at any time looked upon my brother's attempts to write as anything but "thimblehead bobism." Professor Gates gave Frank confidence in himself, and it was Jack Cosgrave's recognition of his ability which resulted in his establishing himself. I very much fear he would have turned out to be a conspicuous failure in the wholesale jewelery business had it not been for the encouragement of these two men. I may record here that Frank often asserted, and with considerable feeling, that in the English*

courses he took at the University of California—
and he majored in English and French—he received no word of recognition, neither guidance
nor helpful criticism. The years he spent there
in attempting to equip himself for a literary
career, he considered practically wasted.

One more word: at no time in his life did
Frank take either himself or his work too seriously. He was highly diverted when sometimes I
called him "the boy Zola." Writing for him was
self-expression. He said once: "Happiness in this
world is being able to devote all your time to the
work you love ; nothing else matters." He never
thought he had exceptional talent, or that he was
in any way unusual. He was as much pleased,
even toward the very end of his life, at a critic's
praise as a school boy over an unexpected prize.
He was ingenious, unaffected and joyful over his
success, and, I suspect, never more so than during
the two years-and-a-half, practically three, when
he was contributing editor to The Wave.

Contents

Frank Norris of *The Wave*

Frank Norris of The Wave & Introduction

BY OSCAR LEWIS

In "Blix," Frank Norris's short novel, which was published in 1899, the leading male character is Condy Rivers, a young San Franciscan with literary ambitions who is associate editor of the Sunday magazine section of the Daily Times. The story is Norris's one venture into the field of the "light" novel, and it is not today considered one of his best works. However, it presents an excellent picture of the young journalist, Rivers, as he hurries about the city covering assignments for his paper: now to the waterfront to do a story of a whaleback steamer loading wheat for the Orient, now to the life-saving station in the Presidio, now haunting curious Mexican restaurants or exploring the cluttered streets of Chinatown. Rivers was born in Chicago and came West with his parents in the early '80s. He attended the State University at Berkeley and, after a finishing year at Yale, made a connection with the San Francisco paper. "For Condy," wrote Norris, "had developed a taste and talent for writing. Short stories were his mania. He had begun

*by an inoculation of the Kipling virus, had suffered
an almost fatal attack of Harding Davis, and had even
been affected by Maupassant." Condy saw life exclu-
sively in terms of "ideas" and "plots" and "points"
for stories. He was bombarding the offices of Eastern
magazines with manuscripts, and he spent hours each
night adding sheet after sheet to a tall rectangle of
manuscript at his elbow. For, of course, he was writing a novel.*

*That "Blix" was very largely autobiographical was at
once recognized in San Francisco when the book was
published. Condy Rivers of the* Daily Times *was in
all important respects Frank Norris of* The Wave;
*Norris as he pictured himself half humorously during
the months before he left for the East and began his
abrupt, skyrocket ascent to fame.*

II.

Frank Norris's connection with The Wave *began in
1891 when a short story, "The Jongleur of Taillebois,"
was printed in the Christmas Number of the weekly.
This was followed in the Midsummer Number of 1892
by "The Way of the World." The author was then a
student at the University of California. Both stories
were highly creditable performances for a youth of
twenty-two. Young Norris's name did not appear
again in the files of* The Wave *until a year and a
half later; then, in the Christmas Number of 1893,*

came a third story, an ironical study of a scheming woman, entitled "Unequally Yoked."

Another two years slipped by before Frank Norris again contributed to the weekly. Meantime, he had completed his four years at Berkeley (failure to make satisfactory grades in mathematics prevented his graduating) and had spent a productive year at Harvard under Professor L. E. Gates. His formal training over, he returned to San Francisco to begin the difficult task of establishing himself. He was then twenty-five and had already written most of the novel that, four years later, was to bring him his first real fame. "McTeague," however, was still unknown in 1895 and, aside from a few stories in California magazines and a now little known book of verse, he had received no recognition. By this time he had abandoned his early ambition to be an artist, although he had continued to make drawings, chiefly illustrations for his own stories and sketches, until he left Berkeley. In 1893 he made a series of illustrations for the college annual, the Blue and Gold, *of which he was art editor. A few other drawings were published elsewhere and may still be encountered in California magazines of the early '90s.*

After a few months in San Francisco he again set off, this time on a journalistic tour of South Africa. It was his hope that the travel sketches he planned to write would pay his expenses and establish magazine connections that would help him with his later work.

In neither respect was his trip an entire success. A few articles in the San Francisco Chronicle *and one in* Harper's Weekly *comprise the total of the African material he was able to place, except for several brief sketches contributed later to* The Wave. *This African journey later had a tragic result, for the fever contracted there wrecked his health and was a contributing factor in the illness that, six years later, resulted in his death.*

Young Norris was still ill when he returned to California in the spring of 1896, and it was probably with the idea of recuperating that he paid a long visit to a friend at a mountain mining camp north of Colfax. The uncompleted manuscript of "McTeague" accompanied him and there he wrote its final chapters. Readers of "McTeague" will recall the incident of the dentist's flight to the mountains after the murder of Trina. McTeague returned to the mine where he had worked as a boy and entered the office to ask for work. "The dentist approached the counter and leaned his elbows upon it. Three men were in the room. . ." One of these was "—a tall, lean young man, with a thick head of hair surprisingly gray, who was playing with a half-grown great Dane puppy. . ." The tall, lean young man was Norris himself, seen through the eyes of his chief character. It was another self-portrait, written only a few weeks before he joined the staff of The Wave.

Introduction
III.

In view of the fact that his massive novel, "The Octopus," dealt largely with the iniquities of the Southern Pacific Railroad, it is interesting to know that the paper on which Norris served his literary apprenticeship was catalogued in San Francisco as a "railroad sheet." By "the railroad" was meant, of course, the Southern Pacific and its president, Collis P. Huntington. The paper had originally been started at Del Monte by Ben Truman of the publicity staff of the Southern Pacific; its chief purpose was to popularize and to promote travel to the new Del Monte Hotel. Later it was transferred to San Francisco and converted into a weekly. This was done with Huntington's help and for the purpose of combating the attacks on himself and his policies that had been launched by other weeklies after he had ousted Stanford from the presidency of the railroad. Its editors were two young newspapermen, J. O'Hara Cosgrave and Hugh Hume. The paper was entertainingly written and shortly became self-supporting; though it continued to support Huntington and his policies to the end, which came shortly after the latter's death in 1900.

Whatever its backing, The Wave during its heyday was a real force in San Francisco journalism. J. O'Hara Cosgrave (his partner, Hugh Hume, withdrew after four years) was a resourceful editor and at no time was his paper a mere vehicle for propaganda. Entering

*an already crowded field, the struggle for recognition
was necessarily a difficult one. On the editorial staffs
of rival papers was then the brilliant group of journalists that included Frank Pixley, Arthur McEwen,
George Fitch, and Ambrose Bierce; all were adepts in
that particularly rough-and-tumble type of personal
journalism then at its height in the West. Into this
truculent company The Wave shouldered its way,
giving as good as it took, and making a place for itself
on its own merits. That place it held for more than a
decade, losing its following only when, toward the beginning of the century, its editor and its more important contributors one by one left San Francisco, attracted by the greater opportunities of the East.*

*The original San Francisco publication office of the
weekly was in two rooms on the second floor of a building at 331 Montgomery Street. In the early '90s it was
housed for a time on O'Farrell Street, just off Market,
from which it presently moved to the Crocker Building, at the corner of Market and Post Streets. In 1896
it moved again, this time across the street to 24 Montgomery Street, where it remained as long as it continued to be published.*

*In its early days, The Wave stressed the social inter-
est and lived up to its subtitle, "A Weekly for Those in
the Swim," in a department, pages long, dealing with
the socially eminent in the immemorial manner of the
society gossip. Gradually, however, the chief emphasis*

swung from society to politics. By 1895 the subtitle had been dropped and the paper had become avowedly a political weekly, playing its forceful and militant part in the now forgotten wrangles that shook the state in the '90s. Its championship of Huntington and the railroad brought it into frequent conflict with the latters' arch-enemies, The Examiner *and* The Argonaut. *These journals were not noted for a tendency to accept criticism in a spirit of meekness, and the exchanges frequently reached the level of personal abuse. This was exactly the type of journalism that San Franciscans most liked, and* The Wave *along with its rivals rode to popularity on the violence of its antagonisms.*

But if the weekly had not presently developed interests other than political and social, it would now be as completely forgotten as some of the other truculent journals of the period. In its early days, outside contributions were seldom printed. The paper was entirely staff-written and it was only in its special Christmas and Midsummer numbers that material from other sources—short stories and sketches by local authors—was used. In these numbers appeared the work of such writers as Bailey Millard, Geraldine Bonner, Juliet Wilbor Tompkins, Ambrose Bierce, Emma Frances Dawson, W. C. Morrow, Arthur McEwen and, beginning in 1891, Frank Norris. Later, it was also to publish the work of another talented group, among them, Will Irwin, James Hopper, Jack London and Gelett Burgess.

IV.

In the issue of October 12, 1895, The Wave *printed "A California Vintage," a description of wine-making in the Santa Clara Valley. It was Frank Norris's first contribution to the paper in almost three years. Then, six months later, in April, 1896, he joined the staff of the weekly as assistant editor, and for the next two years hardly a number appeared that did not contain one or two, and frequently more, contributions signed by him, either with his own name or a pseudonym.*

It was during these two years of his connection with The Wave *that young Norris completed his literary apprenticeship. Writing after the latter's early death, Gelett Burgess referred to his work on the paper as "the studio sketches of a novelist in the making," and Will Irwin who, in 1899, succeeded to Norris's old berth as assistant editor, has written that the latter's stories and sketches for* The Wave *constitute "a study in the way a genius takes to find himself." The editor, Cosgrave, fully recognized the ability of his young friend and assistant, and the latter was given a very free hand in his treatment of the subjects assigned him. Frank Norris made the most of that freedom. Even in a period when the local journalists enjoyed a singularly free rein in the expression of their views, it is doubtful if any of them carried individuality of style and treatment to greater lengths than he.*

Naturally, it was not long before his particularly

realistic type of reporting began to attract the attention of readers of the weekly. Norris's work lent added prestige to the already recognized literary quality of the paper. He wrote whatever chanced to interest him: short stories, dialogues, descriptive articles, interviews, theatrical and art criticisms, editorials, book reviews, parodies, character sketches, translations, and miscellaneous fragments describing colorful phases of San Francisco, the city that perpetually fascinated him. Football was then one of his major enthusiasms and during the fall of 1896 he conducted a department, "The Week's Football," in which he analyzed games and players with all the painstaking thoroughness of the sports writer of today.

Readers of the following pages may judge for themselves the quality of this diverse material that flowed with such rapidity from his pen. It was the work of a young writer of unusual natural talent whose training period was nearing its end and who was pouring forth copy with all the fresh enthusiasm of one who is just beginning to realize his powers. His work had a crisp vitality, a sharply individual viewpoint, that caused even routine assignments to take on a really remarkable interest and significance. Late in 1896, a fifty-ton cannon was towed to Lime Point and dragged up the face of the cliffs to new fortifications at the northern entrance to the Golden Gate. In Norris's hands, the story of this feat became a genuinely thrilling contest

*of man's ingenuity pitted against the inertia of this
"sulky leviathan." A visit to the training quarters of a
football team, a description of the mechanism of a
pipe-organ, the departure of a schooner carrying colo-
nists to the South Seas—all under Norris's treatment
became invested with lively interest and importance.*

V.

*To readers of today, however, these descriptive arti-
cles are less important than his fiction of the same
period. During the twenty-two months of his connection with* The Wave, *more than half his contributions
to the paper were fiction. Short stories, dialogues, character sketches, fragments of description and action appear in almost every number. To the literary student,
these present that always fascinating spectacle of a
first-rate artist undergoing the inevitable period of trial
and experiment before his talent, one might say, crystallizes and he "finds himself."*

It is easy, in the files of The Wave, *to follow his
enthusiasm for other writers of the day, for Kipling,
Richard Harding Davis, Howells, Anthony Hope, and
of course, Emile Zola. Norris, however, was too genuine an artist to accept any of these popular favorites
without reservations; his stories were always indubi-
tably his own; even the earliest of them were too strongly
marked with his own individuality to be mere imita-
tions. The series of amusing parodies reprinted in this*

volume show how carefully and to what good purpose he had read the men of his time who enjoyed big reputations. Only thorough acquaintance with their work could have enabled him so unerringly to catch their style and exaggerate their mannerisms as he did in these clever burlesques.

Of his stories in The Wave, those written in the realistic manner of "McTeague" may today be recognized as of far greater permanent worth. Here his individual talent found its natural outlet; here he was in fact "telling the truth as he saw it, independent of fashion and the gallery gods. . ." What effect some of these Wave stories had on readers of the weekly must, unfortunately, be left to conjecture. One pauses to wonder how unsuspecting subscribers of the mid-'90s received, for instance, the issue of November 6, 1897. In this was published, under the ironical title, "Fantaisie Printaniere," a grim and brutal fragment of slum life, in which the curious names, "McTeague" and "Trina," first appeared in print. This, with such stories as "Judy's Service of Gold Plate"—like "Fantaisie Printaniere," a variation of one of the minor themes in "McTeague"—"Bandy Callaghan's Girl," and the sketches grouped under the title "Western City Types," first informed a few of the discriminating that The Wave was sponsoring a new and powerful talent.

Although the material written in what later came to be recognized as his characteristic manner forms the most important part of his work for The Wave, *Norris's numerous contributions in lighter vein are by no means unworthy of preservation. These reveal a phase of his talent little known to his admirers today. After he became known, he returned to this manner only once, and with not altogether satisfactory results, in the short novel, "Blix." Yet his work for* The Wave *includes much excellent writing in this vein. Such sketches as "A Miner Interviewed," "The Bombardment," and "When a Woman Hesitates," and many of his short dialogues combine humor and satire with a lightness of touch which shows that, had he cared to develop this phase of his talent, he might have won success in quite another field of fiction.*

It is interesting and perhaps significant to note, however, that Norris did not sign his own name to many of these experiments in humor and satire. A considerable number of them were printed under a pseudonym—"Justin Sturgis." Whether he adopted a nom-de-plume *because he felt that these sketches did not represent his best work, or for another reason, is not entirely clear. Originally, the "Justin Sturgis" pseudonym was used when Norris had more than one contribution in the same issue of the weekly; in such cases, the more important story or article was signed with the author's own name and the minor one with the pseudonym. In this way, many of the shorter pieces—which were often brief satirical sketches—came*

*to be signed by "Justin Sturgis," and Norris seems
presently to have adopted this name for all material of
that sort without regard to whether or not he had other
signed contributions in the same issues. Because so
much material was written by Cosgrave and Norris,
both occasionally resorted to pseudonyms to lend variety to the table of contents, and it is no longer possible
in every case to identify the real author.*

*However, there is no question that the "Justin
Sturgis" sketches here reprinted were written by Norris. The individuality of style is in itself sufficient
evidence of authorship, but there is a wealth of other
points that establish the identification beyond question: parallels in subject-matter and viewpoint, dupli-
cation in the use of proper names, the common use of
certain mannerisms in punctuation, and in one case,
an identical reference. In "A Case for Lombroso,"
which appeared under Norris's own name in the issue
of April 11, 1897, occurred this sentence: "You will
remember the fable of Aesop about the two jars . . .
floating in the cistern." Three months later, on July
24, in "The Opinions of Leander," signed by "Justin
Sturgis," was this very similar sentence: "You will,
perhaps, recall the fable of Aesop, of the two jars
floating in the cistern." When Norris left the paper,
early in 1898, the "Justin Sturgis" contributions
likewise ceased to appear.*

VI.

In all, something over 120 Frank Norris contributions appeared in The Wave *between 1891 and 1898. These include everything to which he signed either his name, his initials, or a pseudonym. There is no doubt that he also contributed a great deal of unsigned material, some of which, including several editorials, can be almost certainly identified by their style and content. It has been thought best, however, to avoid including in the present collection anything of which the authorship is even remotely in doubt.*

A considerable amount of the Frank Norris material from The Wave *has already been republished in book form. Ten short stories from the weekly were included in the collection called "The Third Circle," published in 1909, and, in 1906, "Miracle Joyeux," which first appeared in* The Wave *for October 9, 1897, was brought out in a little book with the title, "The Joyous Miracle." In 1928, Charles G. Norris collected a volume of his brother's unrepublished work from magazines and newspapers. This became Volume X of the Argonaut Edition of Frank Norris's works; it contains twenty well-selected contributions from* The Wave. *The latter were located only after much difficulty, for the weekly had suspended publication more than a quarter of a century before and most of the copies that had chanced to be preserved were destroyed in the San Francisco fire of 1906.*

Long runs of The Wave *are now very rarely encountered and no complete file is known to be in existence. The material in the present volume was selected from a file from which only a few numbers are missing, which has been assembled over a period of years by a San Francisco collector. Except for about twenty contributions (mostly reviews and articles, and all of minor importance) the material on the following pages makes available to readers the last of the unrepublished Frank Norris material from* The Wave.

On January 8, 1898, the weekly published the first installment of a novel by its assistant editor. The story continued through thirteen consecutive numbers, ending with the issue of April 9. Before the end was reached, however, the serialized chapters of "Moran and the Lady Letty" had accomplished what the manuscript of "McTeague" had failed to do; that is, had brought its author to the attention of an Eastern publishing firm. Frank Norris was summoned to New York, and "Moran," after re-serialization in the New York Tribune, *was brought out in book form late in 1898. "McTeague" and "Blix" followed the next year and, in 1901, appeared his great achievement, "The Octopus." In less than three years after he had left* The Wave *young Norris had won a position in the first rank of American novelists—a position which he maintained and consolidated until, late in 1902, his career was abruptly terminated by death.*

Bandy Callaghan's Girl

A SHORT STORY *from* **The Wave** *of April* 18, 1896.

This story is about a certain street-car conductor named Bandy Callaghan. It all happened because of a Chinaman, who once rode on Bandy's car and in some way managed to cheat him out of five dollars. Bandy had to make good the amount at the "Old Man's" office, but he remembered that his Chinaman was marked with leprosy in a peculiar way, and so filled a piece of rubber hose with sand and hid it in the lamp-box against the possibility of meeting him again.

Some time after this Bandy got the receiver of his bell-punch plugged with punch-wads, and took it down to a gunsmith's on Kearny Street not far from the old Plaza to have it cleaned. As he could not call for it until he was off duty, about midnight, he arranged to have the gunsmith leave it at a neighboring saloon. When it was finished Bandy called for it there and started home, taking a short cut through Chinatown. According to his system of reckoning it was 12:27, for, if you will notice, a conductor always tells you the time with great exactness as to the minutes.

On the corner of Washington and Dupont, under a lamp-post, he caromed against a Chinese with traces of leprosy across his nose and eyes like a pair of spectacles. Bandy grabbed him at once by the slack of his blouse.

"Gi' me my five dollars," he said, breathing through his nose. "I knew I'd find you again some day."

The Chinaman wrenched back from him and his lip drew tight across his teeth.

"Wha's mäar 'you?" he snarled. "I no sabe you. Wha's you want, you?"

"I want my five dollars," answered Bandy, taking a fresh hold, "an' I want it quick."

"Wha's mäar 'you?" repeated the other angrily, "I no sabe you fi' dollar. Wha's mäar 'you?" and he called Bandy a bad name which is the first English expression that a Chinaman learns. Bandy had his arm crooked to strike, when the coolie slipped away from him like a lizard and fled up Dupont Street toward Jackson; Bandy reached after him, missed him, and then gave chase.

Now, it is not good to try to run down a Chinaman in Chinatown at night, and none but a detective who has made the quarter a study should ever attempt it. In the first place you are not likely to catch your man, and in the second you are very likely to get into trouble. Bandy, because he did not know the rules of the game in Chinatown and because he was very close

A short story published in The Wave *of April* 18, 1896.

A short story published in The Wave *of April 18, 1896.*

to the thief and because he was bent upon getting back his five dollars, closed in upon the coolie's tracks, followed around the corner of Jackson Street, and as he dodged down a miserable alley a few doors above Dupont, turned in after him, scarcely three yards behind.

Bandy's man dived into a door that looked like the entrance to a tan-room and slammed it behind him, but Bandy's foot was already between the door and the jamb, he flung the door open again and continued the pursuit down the corridor that ended at the head of a long flight of narrow stairs leading down into inky obscurity. It seemed like wilful self-destruction to go on now, but five dollars are five dollars when you get them by hourly installments of twenty-two cents, and besides Bandy was so close to the fleeing coolie that he thought to overtake him at every step.

More stairways and galleries, passageways so low that Bandy had to bow his head to proceed, so narrow that at times he was obliged to advance sideways. Then he paused, panting for breath in the fetid reek of the underground atmosphere. He had lost his coolie, and now was lost himself.

Then all in a moment he grew thoroughly frightened and desperate; he plunged back through the maze of passages that were like tunnels in a mine, with his arms outstretched and with the readiness to fight a death-fight with any one who opposed him. In the

A short story published in The Wave *of April* 18, 1896.

darkness he stumbled down a pair of steps and fell against a green-painted door, with an iron-latticed hole near its top. The door was unfastened, and yielded as he struck it. He pitched forward into a very small and dimly lighted room, but sprang up in an instant looking about, his teeth and fists shut tight.

The room was a little larger than an ocean-liner's stateroom, and like a stateroom was surrounded on three sides by tiers of bunks. Besides these, there were two mattresses on the floor, and on a very low teak-wood table in the middle of the room were an American student's lamp, with a green shade, and a tray full of pipes. The whole place was full of a pungent blue haze of smoke. There were three Chinamen asleep in as many of the bunks, and on one of the mattresses a fourth was "coiled," half stupefied and lazily smoking. Bandy had stumbled into an opium den in full blast.

The sleepers awoke and bundled themselves out upon the floor, and he on the mattress reached out for the lamp. Bandy kicked his hand away and drew the lamp toward him. They all crowded together in one corner, blinking and chattering; one of them cried out to him and said: "You no take-um lock-up; find-um boss, take-um boss, we no sabe, you go find boss, all same take-um boss."

Bandy was puzzled; they evidently thought that this was a raid, and that he was a policeman, but

A short story published in The Wave of April 18, 1896.

Bandy Callaghan's Girl

why? Ah! exactly, he knew now; his conductor's uniform with its blue cloth and brass buttons; he was thinking very fast and felt that he must act on every thought; he could not afford to hesitate, letting them have time to discover their mistake, he was sure that he was master of the situation and his fear and excitement began to subside.

"Here you," he said, addressing the one that spoke, "I want *you*, come outside into the street with me, go on first and I'll follow you." He had thought by this means to regain the street without letting them know that he was lost and was about to follow the coolie, who had gone out before him, when he stopped short with an exclamation.

His first thought had been that it was another Chinaman, too far gone to wake up with the others. His next, (induced by the sight of a quantity of black hair tumbled about upon the pillow) was that a Chinese woman had found her way to the den and lay there on the mattress drugged and inert. But now the figure stirred, breathed heavily, and threw a bare arm free of the blankets. Bandy shrank back with an oath as he saw that the arm was white.

The horror and cruelty of the thing for a moment turned him cold, and then all his excitement came over him again like a hot wave. He was persuaded the coolies were afraid of him. "Here's what I wanted," he cried; "come back here. This girl's got to go out with me."

*A short story
published in*
The Wave *of*
April 18, 1896.

They were silent for a moment and then they all
rushed together, chattering angrily and stood between
him and the door. Without knowing how it had been
done, Bandy found that he had wrapped the girl in the
blankets. Now he stood and faced them, with one arm
supporting her as she leaned limply against him.

Bandy was a young man of limited education and
highly colored imagination, apt to take things that
happened to him as though they were the scenes of a
drama in which he was at once the actor, the author,
and the audience. Through all his hurry and excitement he found occasion to appreciate the drama of the
present situation and felt heroic at once. It stood him
in good stead. He was unwilling to back down now
lest it should destroy the effect. With a quickness of
eye that was born of the occasion he saw one of the
coolies groping toward something on the ground near
his feet. Looking down he saw that it was his nickel-
plated bell-punch, fallen from his pocket during the
moment he was upon the floor, at the same time he
knew that the coolie had mistaken it for something
else; he did not undeceive him but snatched it up and
aimed it at them, shouting:

"It's a forty-eight and it's loaded to the muzzle,
damn you all, stand out of the way." They fell back
before him and he blundered out into the narrow passage carrying the girl with him.

Behind him he heard the sound of a shrill whistle,

A short story published in The Wave *of April 18, 1896.*

and shriller voices calling to each other up and down the tortuous stairways. He went on through the foul murk in a frenzy of excitement speaking all his thoughts aloud, as was his custom when aroused, ignorant of where he was going, and possessed of only one desire—to get above ground again and breathe the clear night air.

And then all his courage and resolution suddenly dwindled away and left him cold and shaking with fear. He knew that he was only a car conductor after all, and had neither the blind recklessness of the tough nor the reasoned obstinacy of the thoroughbred. With every minute of continued suspense he began to think less of the girl and more of himself. The idea of being set upon by Chinamen in that narrow tunnel, like a rat in its hole, filled him with terror, and he raised his voice in a quavering shout for help. He paused a moment and listened; a rising clamor in the gloom behind him prolonged the echo of his cry, while in front of him he heard the noise of feet descending a flight of invisible stairs. It seemed as though he were trapped. The strain of waiting there in the dark for the blow to fall was more than he was made to bear, so letting the girl slip from his grasp, he started forward with another shout and ran with outstretched arms against the blue-coated figure of a policeman upon the stairs in front of him.

At sight of the white face and at sound of the bass

A short story published in The Wave *of April* 18, 1896.

voice growling, "What was the matter down here *this time*," Bandy's nerves snapped like a tense harp string, and he burst into weak tears, partly of pure nervousness, partly of joy at his release, partly of shame at his own cowardice, and partly because he had not been able to sustain the heroic role he had assumed.

Five minutes later he was much calmer, and in company with the girl, who was still unconscious, was being driven to the precinct station house in the patrol wagon.

*　*　*

Bandy had a "girl" whose name was Miss McCleaverty, and who ran the soda water fountain in a candy store on Polk Street. Miss McCleaverty wore very blonde hair, and imitation alligator skin belts. She exhaled alternate odors of sachet and chocolate caramels, and she knew how to play "My Lady's Bower" and "The Liberty Bell March" on the piano. Bandy thought her radiantly beautiful and divinely gifted.

The next time that Bandy went to see Miss McCleaverty, he told her all about it and was puzzled at her lack of enthusiasm and interest in the matter. She did not seem to care much about the thrilling details, and spoke carelessly of the girl as "this woman," which made him wince. But he finally got her promise to go with him and see the girl at the "Home."

At the "Home" it was quite different, however. As

*A short story
published in
The Wave of
April 18, 1896.*

soon as she saw the forlorn little creature, Miss Mc-Cleaverty warmed toward her in a way that filled Bandy's simple heart with joy. She sat with her arm around her a long time, got her to talk a little, and left her with the assurance that she would come and see her again as soon as she could.

By the time Bandy saw Miss McCleaverty again she had been out to the "Home" twice, and had found out more about the Girl. "I guess she's Mexican-Spanish," she said to Bandy, " 'n it ain't altogether her fault that she's what she is; of course she won't tell me everything, but she's got people in San Diego; 'n there was a fellow—I don't know—'n they ran away together, 'n he didn't do right by her. He left her after awhile, 'n then, well, she met a woman, 'n you know she's awfully young 'n ain't onto herself a little bit, 'n the woman did worse by her than the fellow, 'n she just went all to pieces. But you just bet I'm going to stand right by her 'n get her back to her folks, all right, all right."

"You didn't seem to be stuck on her much at first," observed Bandy.

"Well, I know," assented Miss McCleaverty, vaguely. "But she ain't got a friend in the whole city, 'n she ain't a bit bad, just kinda weak 'n inexperienced, you know. She's just awfully sorry about everything, 'n I mean to help her get set straight again. I tell you what," she went on, "that Home ain't a very nice

A short story published in The Wave of *April 18, 1896.*

place for her, b'cause she ain't one of that kind. My aunt was in the store yesterday, 'n I told her all about it, 'n she felt just as I did. She's going to let her come to stay with her until we get word from her folks. She lives way out on Geary Street, you know; she's all alone, 'n it's kinda lonesome like, anyhow."

"Well, say, that's pretty nice," said Bandy, "and it's just awfully good of you. Say, did she ever say anything about me?"

"No," answered Miss McCleaverty. "I guess she's got too many other things to think about."

"She's mighty pretty, don't you think?"

Miss McCleaverty shifted her gum to the other side of her mouth. "I wouldn't call her pretty at all," she responded.

Some time after this Bandy awoke to the fact that he had been visiting at the house on Geary Street as often as he could, and that after one of these visits he spent most of his time in looking forward to the next one. There was little enough that he had in common with the Girl, and heaven knows what they talked about. He thought that he had liked Miss McCleaverty more than any one else, but now he began to see that he had never known what it really meant to care for some one.

"This must be what it is," he said, "when people fall in love."

He felt mortified, too, over the fact that he was un-

Bandy Callaghan's Girl

A short story published in The Wave *of April* 18, 1896.

faithful to Miss McCleaverty, who had been so kind to him.

"She ain't done anything," he observed, to himself, "but I just can't help it."

It came to be tacitly felt between himself and the Girl that Miss McCleaverty should know nothing of his visits, and this mutual understanding seemed in a way to draw them closer together. He began to perceive as well that the Girl was commencing to care for him, but this troubled him as much as it rejoiced him, for he felt that they were not fated for each other, and that no good could come of it all. Meanwhile Miss McCleaverty saw nothing, but continued to do all that she could for her. After a while she succeeded in getting her to tell her all about her parents and had written to them at San Diego; but Bandy could scarcely bear to look Miss McCleaverty in the face.

How the Girl had come into the opium den underneath the tan-shop in St. Louis Place Bandy never knew. It was more than likely she did not know herself, though he was sure she had not been there often. They never spoke of that night between themselves, and Bandy often wondered if she knew what part he had taken in the business.

The house, which was the Girl's temporary home, was far out on Geary Street, and close under Lone Mountain. Late one afternoon, when their acquain-

A short story published in **The Wave** *of April* 18, 1896.

tance was three weeks old, Bandy went out there again as he had done so many times already. As he rang the bell, a woman in the adjoining house, who was watering some geraniums at her open window, called to him, saying:

"Mrs. Flint (this was Miss McCleaverty's aunt) told me as how I was to tell you if you called, that she had gone out and wouldn't be home till late this evening, but the young lady's at home; I guess you can walk right in."

The house was a small one and all on one floor, and Bandy shut the front door sharply behind him, so that the noise might announce his coming. He went into the little front sitting-room and moved about uncertainly, waiting till the Girl should come in. The house was so small that she could not help hearing him. He waited some few minutes, touching the keys of the cheap piano and whistling softly. Then, after a few moments' hesitation, he returned to the entry and called. There was no answer, and he turned back to the sitting-room, assured that she was not in the house. But the next moment he was persuaded of the improbability of this; she never went out under any circumstances, having an unreasonable dread of being seen abroad. Yet in the bare possibility of her having stirred out of doors for once, he sat down and waited for upwards of half an hour.

At the end of this time he jumped up impatiently;

A short story published in The Wave *of April* 18, 1896.

it was growing dark, and. he was positive she would not have stayed out so long, even if she had gone out at all.

"Can't be," he muttered; "she must be at home." For a second time he went out into the hall and called loud and long, with only latent echoes for response. Her room was at the end of the hall and he could see her door from where he stood. He went up to it and knocked, and then, receiving no answer, tried the knob. The door was locked. "This is getting queerer and queerer," he said, but he was uneasy as he spoke the words. As he turned away perplexed and hesitating, the noise of running water caught his ear; it came from within the room, and was as the noise of water running from the faucet of a stationary wash-stand. Not knowing what to think, he took a couple of turns up and down the hallway, his hands thrust deep in his pockets and his eyebrows knotted in a puzzled frown. The noise of the trickling stream followed him back and forth. It was the only sound throughout the house. "It sounds leery," he said to himself.

Returning to the door, he pulled out his bunch of keys from his pocket and tried one of them in the lock, and drew back in astonishment. The key was on the inside.

"This is funny, too," he muttered, more and more uneasy. "There's no other way out of the room, and how could any one go off and leave that water running, and lock the door from the inside."

A short story published in The Wave *of April* 18, 1896.

He started up suddenly and looked about him, bewildered and excited, drawing his breath quickly.

"Say, there's something wrong; I've got to get into that room."

He worried the key in the door loose with the butt of his pencil, and pushed it till it fell from the lock on the inside of the room. Before he tried again to fit one of his own keys to the lock, he bent down and peered through the keyhole. Then, as he did so, his heart jumped to his throat with a great bound, and stuck there quivering, and he sprang up, beating his hands together, crying out again and again. He had seen nothing in the room, but through the narrow vent of the keyhole was streaming a strangling odor of escaping gas.

For a moment in a frenzy of alarm and excitement he ran back in the front of the house, biting at the ends of his fingers and talking aloud to himself. A pair of disused Indian-clubs stood in one corner of the sitting-room. He caught up one of these and running back to the room splintered the door into long fragments in half a dozen blows.

Inside it was like breathing a vaporous brass, the poisoned air closed around him, and filled his lungs and breast and throat till it seemed as though he must suffocate before he could even reach the window on the other side of the room. It was partly open; he flung it higher still, and turned to the interior of the room. But though there was evidence that she had been there but recently, it was now empty.

He shut off the water and the escaping gas, and sat down on the window edge, bewildered, and gasping for air. Where could the girl have gone? What was the meaning of it all? He glanced around the room for an explanation. His eyes rested on a little table at the bed-side and on it he saw something that explained it all: a little silver pipe and a half-empty package of unboiled opium. That was it, then: unwittingly, she had contracted the dreadful habit, had struggled against it, no doubt, since her rescue, and had succumbed to it at last, had turned on the gas, perhaps accidentally, in the course of her stupor, perhaps with design in a moment of remorse and grief and conscious helplessness, and then drugged by the poisonous fumes and equally poisonous smoke had wandered away into the night. How? Through the window. It was not four feet above the level of the ground; and swinging himself out Bandy saw the print of her feet in the soil.

And where now had she gone? What might not happen to her in her helpless condition?

Lone Mountain is one of the most conspicuous landmarks in the city, because it rises very abruptly and very steeply from the surrounding streets and because there are no other hills or tall buildings near by to obscure it. Being thus steep and abrupt there

A short story published in The Wave *of April* 18, 1896.

are no houses upon it and no streets, nothing but goat-paths and scrubby bushes, all covered with the red dust of the streets which the trade-winds blow there. There is a great wooden cross upon the top. It was a pretty idea to place it there, because you may see the mountain from almost anywhere in the city, and the cross upon it stands there in its simple isolation, sometimes clear-cut and black against the sun going redly down through the Golden Gate, sometimes blurred and indistinct in the rains and in the fogs, or sometimes silvery with great black shadows in the moonlight; but always there, looking far out over the city, its great arms stretched wide as though in protection and benison.

The house stood at the very foot of the mountain, and Bandy had not taken half a dozen steps into the night—for it was quite dark by this time—before he felt the slope rise under his feet.

By a sudden unreasoned instinct he knew where the Girl had gone, and ran scrambling and panting up the side and paused on the summit.

Below him, the city shrank away and spread out like an unrolled scroll, a blue-gray mass, pierced with many chimney-stacks, that were like the pipes of a great organ, on the unseen keys of which were forever sounded all the notes in the gamut of human happiness and human misery, that united in a single minor chord and rolled upward day and night toward the

A short story published in The Wave of *April 18, 1896.*

great and moveless cross with its outstretched arms.

The Girl was lying in the shadow of the cross, her hands reaching toward it and spread out before her, and her face bowed upon the ground. She must have died where she had fallen.

Bandy saw her as she lay thus, far above the turmoil and dirt of the city's streets and in a better air—one that was purer and calmer. She seemed, as she lay, to be quieter and more content than ever before. Above her towered the great cross with its outstretched arms of protection and benison.

Bandy told this story to me some time afterward, when its impressiveness had worn off and he could bear to talk about it. When he had finished telling it, he extended his remarks in comment:

"I don't know," he said, reflectively, "I thought a good deal of that girl at the time, and I guess I made an awful fool of myself over her. And when she died, oh, you don't know—it hurt. I tell you it hurt *bad*. I thought that I just naturally never *would* get over it. But I did get over it you see. Oh yes, I got over it, but just the same there is always something—when I think of it, somehow it makes my throat ache. It's funny, ain't it?"

"But," said I, "where do *you* come in? What was there in it for *you*? What have *you* got left out of it?"

"Oh!" answered Bandy, "I got Miss McCleaverty."

His Sister

A SHORT STORY FROM

The Wave *of November* 28, 1896.

"Confound the luck," muttered young Strelitz in deep perplexity as he got up from the supper table and walked over to the mantelpiece, pulling at his lower lip as was his custom when thinking hard.

Young Strelitz lived in a cheap New York flat with his mother, to whose support he contributed by writing for the papers.

Just recently he had struck a vein of fiction that promised to be unusually successful. A series of short stories—mere sketches—which he had begun under the title "Dramas of the Curbstone," had "caught on," and his editor had promised to take as many more of them as he could write for the Sunday issue. Just now young Strelitz was perplexed because he had no idea for a new story. It was Wednesday evening already, and if his stuff was to go into the Sunday's paper it should be sent to the editor by the next day's noon at the latest.

"Blessed if I can dig up anything," he exclaimed as he leaned up against the mantelpiece, his forehead in a pucker.

A short story published in The Wave *of* *November 28, 1896.*

He and his mother were just finishing their supper. Mrs. Strelitz brushed the crumbs from her lap and pushed back her chair, looking up at her son.

"I thought you were working on something this afternoon," she hazarded.

"It don't come out at all," he answered, as he drew a new box of cigarettes from his coat pocket. "It's that 'Condition of Servitude' stuff, and I can't make it sound natural."

"But that's a true story," exclaimed Mrs. Strelitz. "That really happened."

"That don't help matters any if it don't read like real life," he returned, as he opened the box of cigarettes. "It's not the things that have really happened that make good fiction, but the things that read as though they had."

"If I were you," said his mother, "I would try an experiment. You've been writing these 'Dramas of the Curbstone' without hardly stirring from the house. You've just been trying to imagine things that you think are likely to happen on the streets of a big city after dark, and you've been working that way so long that you've sort of used up your material—exhausted your imagination. Why don't you go right out—now —to-night, and keep your eyes open and watch what really happens, and see if you can't find something to make a story out of, or at least something that would suggest one. You're not listening, Conrad, what's the matter?"

His Sister

A short story published in The Wave *of November* 28, 18--

It was true, young Strelitz was not listening. The box of cigarettes he had drawn from his pocket was a fresh one. While his mother was talking he had cut the green revenue stamp with his thumb nail, and had pushed open the box, had taken out a cigarette and had put it between his lips.

The box was one of those which contain, in addition to the cigarettes themselves the miniature photograph of some bouffe actress, and Strelitz had found in his box one that was especially debonnaire. But as he looked at the face of the girl it represented he suddenly shifted his position and turned a little pale. He thrust the box back into his pocket, but closed his fist over the photograph as though to hide it. He did not light his cigarette.

"What's the matter, Conrad; you are not listening?"

"Oh, yes I am," he answered. "I—nothing. I'm listening. Go on."

"Well, now, why don't you try that?"

"Try what?"

"Go out and look for a story on the streets."

"Oh, I don't know."

Without attracting his mother's attention, Strelitz looked again at the cigarette picture in his hand and then his glance went from it to a large crayon portrait that stood on a brass easel in the adjoining parlor. The crayon portrait was the head and bare shoulders of a young girl of seventeen or eighteen.

A short story published in The Wave *of* ovember 28, 1896.

The resemblance to Strelitz and his mother was unmistakable, but there was about the chin and the corners of the eyes a certain recklessness that neither of the others possessed. The mouth too was weak.

"You get right down to your reality then," continued Mrs. Strelitz. "Even if you do not find a story, you would find at least a background—a local color that you can observe much better than you can imagine."

"Yes, yes," answered Strelitz. He lounged out of the dining-room, and going into the little parlor turned up the gas, and while his mother and the hired girl cleared away the table, fell to studying the two likenesses—the crayon portrait and the cigarette picture, comparing them with each other.

There was no room for doubt. The two pictures were of the same girl.

However, the name printed at the bottom of the cigarette picture was not that which young Strelitz expected to see.

"Violet Ormonde," he muttered, reading it. "That's the stage-name she took. Poor Sabina, poor Sabina, to come to this." He looked again at the photograph of the bouffe actress, in her false bull-fighter's costume, with its low-necked, close-fitting bodice, its tights, its high-laced kid shoes, its short Spanish cloak and foolish inadequate sword—a sword *opéra comique.* "Poor little girl," he continued under his

A short story published in The Wave *of November* 28, 18

breath as he looked at it, "she could have returned to us if she'd wanted to before she came to this. She could come back now. But where could one find her? What's become of her by this time?"

He was roused by the entrance of his mother and faced about, hastily thrusting the little photograph into his pocket and moving away from the crayon portrait on the brass easel, lest his mother should see him musing over it.

"Conrad," said Mrs. Strelitz, "you don't want to miss a week with your stories now that people have just begun to read them."

"I know," he admitted, "but what can I do? I haven't a single idea."

"Well, now, just do as I tell you. You try that. Go down town and keep your eyes open and see if you can't see something you can make a story out of. Make the experiment, anyhow. You'll have the satisfaction of having tried. Why, just think, in a great city like this, with thousands and thousands of people, all with wholly different lives and with wholly different interests—interests that clash. Just think of the stories that are making by themselves every hour, every minute. There must be hundreds and hundreds of stories better than anything ever yet written only waiting for some one to take them down. Think of how near you may have come to an interesting story and never know it."

A short story published in The Wave *of November* 28, 1896.

His Sister

"That's a good saying, that last," observed young Strelitz, smiling in approval. "I'll make a note of that."

But his note-book was not about him, and rather than let his mother's remark slip his memory he jotted it down upon the back of the cigarette picture.

"Let's see, how does that go?" he said, writing. " 'Think of how close one may come to an interesting story and never know it.' Well," added young Strelitz as he slipped the bit of cardboard back into his pocket. "I'll try your idea, but I haven't much faith in it. However, it won't do any hurt to get in touch with the real thing once in a while. I may get a suggestion or two."

"You may have an adventure or two," observed Mrs. Strelitz.

"Do the Haroun-al-Raschid act, hey?" answered her son. "Well, don't sit up for me," he went on, shrugging himself into his overcoat, " 'cause if I get an idea I may go right up to the 'Times' office and work it up in the reporters' room. Good night."

For more than two hours young Strelitz roamed idly from street to street. Now in the theater district, now in the slums and now in the Bowery. As a rule he avoided the aristocratic and formal neighborhoods, knowing by instinct that he would be more apt to find undisguised human nature along the poorer unconventional thoroughfares.

Hundreds of people jostled him, each with a hidden

*A short story
published in
The Wave of
November 28, 18*

story no doubt; but all such as varied from the indistinguishable herd, resolved themselves into types, hackneyed over-worked types, with nothing original about them. There was the Bowery boy; there was the tough girl; there was the young lady from the college settlement; there was the dude, the chippy, the bicycle girl, the tenement house Irish woman, the bum, the drunk, the policeman, the Chinese laundry man, the coon in his plaid vest and the Italian vegetable man in his velvet jacket.

"I know you, I know you all," muttered young Strelitz, as one after another passed him. "I know you, and you, and you. There's Chimmie Fadden, there's Cortlandt Van Bibber, there's Rags Raegen, there's George's Mother, there's Bedalia Herodsfoot, and Gervaise Coupeau and Eleanor Cuyler. I know you, every one; all the reading world knows you. You're done to death; you won't do, you won't do. Nothing new can be got out of you, unless one should take a new point of view, and that couldn't be done in a short story. Let's go into some of their saloons."

He entered several of the wine shops in the Italian quarter, but beyond the advertisement of a public picnic and games, where the second prize was a ton of coal, found nothing extraordinary.

"Now we'll try the parks," he said to himself. He turned about and started across town. As he went on the streets grew cleaner and gayer. The saloons be-

*A short story
published in*
The Wave *of*
November 28, 1896.

came "elegant" bars. The dance halls, brilliantly lighted theaters. Here and there were cafes, with frosted glass, side doors, on which one read "Ladies' Entrance." Invariably there was a cab stand near by.

"Ah, the Tenderloin," murmured Strelitz slackening his pace. "I know you, too. I'll have a cocktail in passing, with you."

A large cafe, whose second story was gayly lighted, attracted him. He entered the bar on the ground floor and asked for a mild cocktail.

All at once he heard his name called. A party of men of his own age stood in the entrance of a little room that opened from the barroom, beckoning to him and laughing. Three of them he knew very well—Brunt of the "Times," Jack Fremont, who had graduated with his class, and Angus McCloutsie, whom every one called "Scrubby." The other men Strelitz knew to bow to. "Just the man we want," cried Jack Fremont as Strelitz came up.

"You're right in time," observed "Scrubby," grinning and shaking his hand. "Come in, come in here with us." They pulled young Strelitz into the little room, and Brunt made them all sit down while he ordered beer.

"We're having the greatest kind of a time," Fremont began in an excited whisper. "All the crowd are upstairs—we got a room, we had supper—there's Dryden and Billy Libbey, and the two Spaulding boys

*A short story
published in*
The Wave *of*
November 28, 189.

and the 'Jay'—and all the old crowd. Y'ought to see
Dick Spaulding sitting on the floor trying to put
gloves on his feet; he says there were seven good reasons why he should not get full and that he's forgotten,
every one. Oh, we're going to have the time of our
lives to-night. You're just in time—"

"Joe's forgot the best part of it," broke in "Scrubby."

"There are three girls."

"Three girls?"

"Yes, sir, and one of them is the kind you read
about. Just wait till you see her."

"I'm not going to wait," said young Strelitz. "I must
go, right away. I'm working to-night." He finished
his beer amongst their protests, and drew his handkerchief quickly out of his pocket and wiped his lips.
But the others would not hear of his going.

"Oh, come along up," urged Brunt. "Just listen to
that," cocking his head toward the ceiling, "and see
what you're missing. That's Dick trying to remember."
Strelitz hesitated. They certainly were having a glorious time up there—and the girls, too. He might at
least go up and look in on them all. He began to re-
flect, pulling at his lower lip, his forehead in a pucker.
If he went up there he would miss his story.

"No, no, I can't fellows," he said decisively, rising
from the table. "I've got to do some work to-night.
Another time I'll join you; you have your good time
without me this once." He pulled away from the re-

*A short story
published in
The Wave of
:ember 28, 1896.*

taining hands that would have held him, and ran out into the street, laughing over his shoulder at them, his hat on the back of his head.

"Well, if he's got to work, he's got to work," admitted "Scrubby," as the swing doors flapped behind young Strelitz.

"He's going to miss the time of his life, though," put in Fremont. "Come on, let's go back to the crowd. What's that you got?"

"It's something that flipped out of Con's pocket, I think, as he pulled out his handkerchief. It's a cigarette picture."

"Some one of Con's fairies? Let's have a look."

They crowded together, looking over each other's shoulders. Suddenly there was an exclamation—

"Why, that's the girl that's upstairs now, the queen— the one that's so drunk. See the name; she said her name was Violet."

"Con must have known her."

"Too bad he had to shake the crowd."

"He would have had a great time with that girl."

"I say, what's he got written on the back?"

In the midst of a great silence, Brunt turned the cigarette picture to the light and read:

"Think how close one may come to an interesting story and never know it."

End of the Beginning ✐

A SHORT STORY FROM
𝔗𝔥𝔢 𝔚𝔞𝔳𝔢 *of September* 4, 1897.

The story of the "Freja" disaster is best told by one or two extracts taken from the record left by Lieutenant Ferriss at Cape Sheridan, and by certain passages from his Ice Journal.

(Extracts of record left in instrument box at Cape Sheridan.)

U. S. Cutter "Freja,"
On the ice off Cape Sheridan, Grant Land,
Lat. 82° 25′ N., Lon. 61° 30′ W., 12th March, 1891.

* * * We accordingly froze the ship in on the last day of September, 1890, and during the following winter drifted with the pack in a northwesterly direction. * * * On Friday, August 2d, being in Lat. 82° 25′ N., Lon. 61° 30′ W., the "Freja" was caught in a severe nip between two floes and was crushed, sinking in about two hours. We abandoned her, saving a hundred days' provisions and all necessary clothing, instruments, etc. * * *

I shall now attempt a southerly march over the ice, and with God's help hope to reach Tasiusak, or fall in with the relief ships or steam whalers on the way. Our party consists of the following eighteen persons. * * *

44

A short story
published in
The Wave of
September 4, 1897.

End of the Beginning

All well with the exception of Mr. Bennett, the chief engineer, whose left hand has been frost-bitten. No scurvy in the party as yet.

Hamilton Ferriss, Lieut. U. S. N.
Commanding "Freja" Arctic Exploring Expedition.

(**Extracts** from Lieutenant Ferriss' Ice Journal, three months later than above.)

June 13, 1891—Monday.—Camped at 4.05 p.m. about one hundred yards from the coast. The ice hereabouts is breaking up fast. If we had not been compelled to abandon our boats—but it is useless to repine. We must look our situation squarely in the face. At noon served out last beef extract, which we drank with some willow tea. Our remaining provisions consist of four-fifteenths pounds pemmican per man, and the rest of the dog meat. Where are the relief ships? We should at least have met the steam whalers long before this.

June 14th—Tuesday.—The doctor amputated Mr. Bennett's other hand to-day. Living gale of wind from S. E. Impossible to march against it in our weakened condition—must camp here till it abates. Made soup of the last of the dog meat this afternoon. Our last pemmican gone.

June 15th — Wednesday. — Everybody getting weaker. Clarke breaking down. Sent Hansen down to the shore to gather shrimps, of which it takes fifteen hundred to fill a gill measure. Supper a spoonful of glycerine and hot water.

A short story
published in
The Wave *of*
September 4, 1897

June 16th — Thursday. — Clarke died during the night. Hawes dying. Still blowing a gale from S. E. A hard night.

June 17th—Friday.—Hawes and Cooley died during early morning. Hansen shot a ptarmigan. Made soup. Dennison breaking down.

June 18th—Saturday.—Buried Hawes and Cooley under slabs of ice. Spoonful of glycerine and hot water at noon.

June 19th—Sunday.—Dennison found dead this morning between Bennett and myself. Too weak to bury him or even carry him out of tent. He must lie where he is. Divine services at 5:30 p.m. Last spoonful of glycerine and hot water.

Ferriss paused in his writing at this point, and, looking up from the page, spoke drearily and in a thick, muffled voice: "How long has this wind been blowing, Bennett?"

"Since last Wednesday," answered the other. "Five days." Ferriss continued his writing:

" * * * Gale blowing steadily for five days. Impossible to move against it in our weakened condition. But to stay here is to perish. God help us. It is the end of everything!"

Ferriss drew a line across the page under the last entry, and, still holding the book in his hand, gazed slowly about the tent.

There were nine of them left—eight huddled to-

A short story published in The Wave of ptember 4, 1897.

gether in that miserable tent—the ninth, Hansen, being down on the shore gathering shrimps. In the strange gloomy half-light that filled the tent, these survivors of the "Freja" looked less like men than like animals. Their hair and beards were long, and seemed one with the fur covering on their bodies. Their faces were absolutely black with dirt, and their limbs were monstrously distended and fat—fat as things bloated and swollen are fat. It was the abnormal fatness of starvation, the irony of misery, the huge joke that Arctic Famine plays upon those whom it afterwards destroys. The men moved about at times on their hands and knees; their tongues were round and slate-colored, like the tongues of parrots, and when they spoke they bit them helplessly.

Near the flap of the tent lay the swollen dead body of Dennison, the naturalist of the expedition. Four of the party dozed, inert and stupefied, in their sleeping-bags. The surgeon and Muck-tu, the Esquimalt dog-master, were in the center of the tent boiling their sealskin foot-nips over a fire built of a broken sledge-runner. Ferriss sat upon an empty water-breaker, using his knee as a desk. Near him, sitting on one of the useless McClintock sledges was Bennett, both of whose hands had been amputated in consequence of frost-bite. A tin spoon had been lashed to the stump of his right wrist.

The tent was full of foul smells. The smell of drugs

A short story published in The Wave *of September* 4, 1897

and mouldy gunpowder, the smell of dirty rags, and of unwashed bodies, the smell of stale smoke, of scorched sealskin, of soaked and rotting canvas that exhaled from the tent cover—every smell but that of food.

Outside, the unleashed wind yelled incessantly, like a sabbath of witches and spun about their pitiful shelter and went rioting on, leaping and somersaulting from rock to rock, tossing handfuls of dry dust-like snow into the air, folly-stricken—insatiate—an enormous mad monster gamboling there in some hideous dance of death, capricious, headstrong, pitiless as a famished wolf.

In front of the tent, and over a ridge of barren rocks, was an arm of the sea dotted over with blocks of ice, careening past silently, while back from the coast and back from the tent and to the north and to the south and to the west stretched the illimitable waste of land—flat, grey, harsh, snow and ice and rock, rock and ice and snow, stretching away there under the sombre sky, forever and forever, gloomy, untamed, terrible, an empty region—the scarred battlefield of chaotic forces, the savage desolation of a primordial world.

"Where's Hansen?" asked Ferriss.

"He's away after shrimps," responded Bennett.

Ferriss' eyes returned to the note-book and rested on the open page thoughtfully.

48

A short story published in The Wave *of ptember* 4, 1897.

"Do you know what I've written here, Bennett?" he asked, adding, without waiting for an answer: "I've written 'It's the end of everything.' "

"I suppose it is," admitted Bennett, looking vaguely about the tent. "Yes, the end of everything. It's come at last. Well?"

There was a silence. One of the men in the sleeping-bags groaned and turned upon his face. Outside the wind lapsed suddenly to a prolonged sigh of infinite sadness, clamoring again upon the instant.

"Bennett," said Ferriss, returning his note-book to the box of records, "it is the end of everything, and just because it is I want to talk to you—to ask you something."

Bennett came nearer. The horrid shouting of the wind deadened the sound of their voices—the others could not hear it, and by now it would have mattered very little to any of them if they had. Ferriss picked up an empty rubber bottle that had contained lime juice, and began fingering it.

"Old man," he commenced, "nothing makes much difference now. In a few hours we shall all be like Dennison here." He tapped the body of the naturalist, who had died during the night. It was already frozen so hard that his touch upon it resounded as if it had been a log of wood. "We shall all be like this pretty soon," continued Ferriss, "but there's a little girl back in the world we left, that I loved—that I cared

A short story published in The Wave *of September 4, 1897.*

for," he added, hurriedly. "I don't know as I can quite make you understand how much I—how much she was to me. I would have asked her to marry me before I came off, if I had been sure of her, but I wasn't sure, and so—well—so I never spoke. She never knew how much I cared, and I never knew if she cared at all. And that's what I want to ask you about. It's Helen Parry. You've known her all your life, and you saw her later than I did. You remember I had to come down to the ship two days before you, about the bilge pumps."

While Ferriss had been speaking the last words, Bennett had been sitting very erect upon the sledge, drawing figures and vague patterns in the fur of his sealskin coat with the tip of the tin spoon. Helen Parry! Ah, yes, Ferriss was right. Bennett had known her all his life, and it was just because of this intimacy that she had come to be so dear to him. It was she who had made everything he did seem worth while. Hardly for a moment had she been out of his thoughts during all that fearful voyage.

"It seems rather foolish," continued Ferriss, turning the rubber bag about and about, "but if I thought she ever cared—for me—in that way, why it would make—this that is coming to us, seem—oh, I don't know—easier to be borne. I say it very badly, but it would not be so hard to die if I thought that little girl loved me—a bit."

50

*A short story
published in
The Wave of
September 4, 1897.*

Bennett was thinking very fast. He wished now that he had overridden Helen's objections, and had allowed her people to announce their engagement before the expedition sailed. He had even half guessed something of this sort. But they two were so happy in their avowed love for each other that they had shut their eyes to everything else. They only knew that they were to be married within a month of Bennett's return. Bennett could never forget that evening when he had said good-bye to her on the porch of the old New Hampshire homestead, and had gone away to join the "Freja." She had kissed him then for the first time, and had put a hand on each shoulder and said to him:

"You must come back, Dick—you must come back to me. Remember, you are everything to me—everything in the world."

"You've known her so well," continued Ferriss, "that I am sure that she, understanding that you were my very best friend, must have said something to you about me. Tell me, did she ever say anything—give you to understand—that she cared for me—that she would have married me if I had asked her?"

Bennett wondered what to say to him. On one hand was Helen, the girl that was to be—that would have been his wife, who loved him and whom he loved. On the other was Ferriss, his chief, his friend, his hero, the man of all others whom he loved, as

A short story published in The Wave *of September 4, 1897*

Jonathan loved David—such a love as can come only upon two men who have lived together, and fought together, and battled with the same dangers, and suffered the same defeats and disappointments. Bennett felt himself in grievous straits. Must he tell Ferriss the bitter truth? Must this final disillusion be added to that long train of others, the disasters, the failures, the disappointments and deferred hopes of all those past months? Must Ferriss die hugging to him this bitterness as well?

"I sometimes thought," observed Ferriss, with a weak smile, "that she did care a little. I've surely seen something like that in her eyes at certain moments. I wish I had spoken. Did she ever say anything to you? Did she ever say she cared for me?"

The thing was too cruel. Bennett shrank from it.

But suddenly an idea occurred to him. Did anything make any difference now? Why not tell his friend that which he wanted to hear, even if it were not the truth? After all that he had suffered why could he not die content at least in this? What did it matter if he spoke? Did anything matter at such a time, when they were all to perish within the next twenty-four hours? Ferriss was waiting for his answer, looking straight into his eyes.

"Yes," said Bennett, "she did say something once."

"What was it?" exclaimed Ferriss, dropping the rubber bag and bending forward.

A short story
published in
The Wave of
September 4, 1897.

End of the Beginning

"We had been speaking of the expedition and of you," answered Bennett, looking fixedly on the bag as it lay on the ground. "I don't know how the subject came up, but it came in very naturally at length. She said—I remember her words perfectly—she said, 'He must come back—you must bring him back to me. Remember, he is everything to me—everything in the world.' "

"She said that?" enquired Ferriss, looking away.

"Yes," answered Bennett. "I remember it. Those were her words."

"Ah!" said Ferriss, with a quick breath; then he added, "I'm glad of that. You haven't an idea how happy I am, Bennett, in spite of everything."

"Oh, yes, I guess I have," assented Bennett.

"No, no, you haven't," replied Ferriss. "How can you have any idea of it? One has to love a little girl like that, Bennett, and have her—and find out—and have things come all right to appreciate it. She would have been my wife after all. I don't know how to thank you, old man. Congratulate me."

He rose a little feebly, holding out his hand. Bennett rose and instinctively extended his arm, but withdrew it suddenly. Ferriss paused abruptly, letting his hand fall to his side, and the two remained there an instant, looking at the stumps of Bennett's arms, the tin spoon still lashed to the right wrist! There was a noise of feet at the flap of the tent.

"It's Hansen," muttered Bennett.

Hansen tore open the flap of the tent.

*A short story
published in*
The Wave *of
September* 4, 189?

Then he shouted to Ferriss: "Three steam whalers off the foot of the floe, sir; boat putting off! What orders, sir?"

Ferriss looked at him stupidly, as yet without definite thought, then:

"What did you say?"

Two of the men in the sleeping-bags, wakened by Hansen's shout, sat up and listened stolidly.

"Steam whalers?" said Bennett, slowly. "Where? I guess not," he added, shaking his head.

Hansen was swaying in his place with excitement. "Three whalers," he repeated, "close in. They've put off—Oh, my God! Listen to that!"

The unmistakable sound of a steamer's whistle, raucous and prolonged, came to their ears from the direction of the coast. One of the men broke into a feeble cheer. The whole tent was rousing up. Again and again came the hoarse, insistent cry of the whistle.

"What orders, sir?" repeated Hansen.

A clamor of voices filled the tent.

Bennett came quickly up to Ferriss, trying to make himself heard.

"Old man, listen!" he cried, with eager intentness. "What I told you—just now—about Helen Parry—I thought—it is all a mistake. You don't understand—"

Ferriss was not listening.

End of the Beginning

A short story published in The Wave *of tember 4, 1897.*

"What orders, sir?" exclaimed Hansen, for the third time.

Ferriss drew himself up.

"Lieutenant Ferriss' compliments to the officer in charge. Tell him there are nine of us left—tell him—oh, tell him anything you damn please." "Boys!" he cried, turning a radiant face to the men in the tent, "make ready to get out of this. We're going home—going home to our sweethearts, boys!"

A drawing by Frank Norris from the University of California Blue and Gold, 1894.

Judy's Service of Gold Plate 〜 〜 〜

A SHORT STORY FROM

The Wave *of October* 16, 1897.

She was a native of Guatemala, and so, of course, was said to be Mexican, and she lived in the alley by the county jail, three or four doors above the tamale factory. Her trade was something odd. The Chinamen, who go down to the sea in ships from San Francisco to Cape St. Lucas, off the coast of Lower California, and fish for sharks there, used to bring the livers of these sharks back to her. She would boil the oil out of these livers and turn over the product to a red-headed Polish Jew named Knubel, who bottled it and sold it to San Francisco as cod liver oil. Knubel made money in the business. She was only his employee. Her name, incidentally, was Lambala Largomarsini, which was no doubt the reason why she was called "Judy."

Knubel lived on Telegraph Hill, on the ledge of the big cliff there, and used to lie awake o' windy nights waiting for his house to be blown off that ledge.

Judy's Service of Gold Plate

A short story published in The Wave *of October 16, 1897.*

Knubel had always lived on Telegraph Hill. When he was forty he had had a stroke of paralysis, and had lost the use of his left leg. The result of this stroke was that Knubel was held a prisoner on the Hill. He dared not go down into the city below him, because he knew he could never get back. How could he, stop and think? No horse ever gets to the top of the Hill. The cable-cars and electric-cars turn their headlights upon the Hill and shake their heads and go around in the valley by Stockton street. The climb is bad enough for a man with two healthy legs, but for a paralytic— Knubel was trapped upon the Hill, trapped and held prisoner. He never saw Kearny or Montgomery or Market streets after his stroke. He never saw the new *Call* building, or the dome upon the City Hall but from afar, and the "Emporium" was to him but a distant granite cliff. In the newspaper, he who lived in San Francisco read about what was happening there as you and I and all the rest of us read about what is happening in London or in Paris or in Vienna, and this with the roar of that San Francisco actually in his ears, like the bourdon of a tremendous organ.

Judy of course was wretchedly poor, for the salary that Knubel allowed her for boiling down the shark's livers would not have fattened a self-respecting chessy-cat. Knubel himself was a horrible old miser, he had made a little fortune in cod liver oil, but he kept it tied up in three old socks in a starch box underneath

*A short story
published in*
The Wave *of
October* 16, 1897

the floor of his cellar. He had a passion for gold, and turned all his silver and greenbacks into gold as fast as he could. He lived in a room about as big as a trunk back of an Italian wine shop where there was a "Bocce" court, and Judy used to come and see him here once a month and get her salary and make her report.

One day when Judy had come to get her orders and her money from Knubel she found him bending his red head over his table testing an old brass collar button with nitric acid.

"I found him bei der stairs on der bottom," he explained to Judy. "Berhaps he is of gold. Hey, yes?"

Judy looked at the collar button.

"That ain't gold," she declared. "Huh! you can't fool me on gold. I seen more gold in my day than you've seen tin, Mister Knubel."

Knubel's eyes were gimlets on the instant.

"Vat you say?"

"When I was a kid in Guatemala my folks had a set of gold plate, dishes you know, hundreds of 'em, all solid gold."

Here we touch on Judy's one mania. She believed and often stated that at one time her parents in Guatemala were enormously wealthy, and in particular were possessed of a wonderful service of gold plate. She would describe this gold plate over and over again to anyone who would listen. Why there were

A short story published in The Wave *of October* 16, 1897.

Judy's Service of Gold Plate

more than a hundred pieces, all solid red gold. Why there were goblets and punch-bowls and platters and wine-pitchers and ladles, why the punch-bowl itself was worth a fortune. Ignorant enough on other subjects, and illiterate enough, Heaven knows, once started on her gold plate, Judy became almost eloquent. Of course, no one believed her story, and rightly so because the gold plate never did exist. How Judy got the idea into her mind it was impossible to say, but it was the custom of people who knew of her mania to set her going and watch her while she rocked to and fro with closed eyes, and hands clasped over her knee chanting monotonously, "More'n a hundred pieces, and all red, red gold," and so on and so on.

For a long while her hearers scoffed, then at last she suddenly made a convert, old Knubel, the red-headed Polish Jew, believed her story on the instant. As often as Judy would come to make her monthly report on the shark liver industry, old Knubel would start her going, swallowing her words as a bullion-bag swallows coin. As soon as Judy had finished he would begin to ask her questions.

"The gold voss soft, hey? und ven you rapped him mit der knuckles now, he rung out didn't he, yes?"

"Sweeter'n church bells."

"Ah, sweeter nor der church bells, shoost soh. I know, *I* know. Now let's have ut egain, more'n a hoondurt bieces. Let's haf ut all *eg*-gain." And again

*A st. . . . ry
published in*
The Wave *of
October* 16, 1897

and again Judy would tell him her wonderful story, delighted that she had at last found a believer. She would chant to Knubel by the hour, rocking herself back and forth, her hands clasped on her knee, her eyes closed. Then by and by Knubel, as he listened to her, caught *himself* rocking back and forth, keeping time with her.

Then Knubel found excuses for Judy's coming to see him oftener than once a month. The manufacture of cod liver oil out of sharks' livers needed a great deal of talking over. Knubel knew her story by heart in a few weeks and began to talk along with her. There in that wretched room over the "Bocce" court on the top of Telegraph Hill, the "Mexican" hybrid woman and the Polish Jew, red-headed and paralytic, rocked themselves back and forth with closed eyes and clasped hands sing-songing, "More'n a hundred pieces, all red, red gold"—"More den a hoondurt bieces und alle rad gold."

It was a strange sight to see.

"Judy," said Knubel, one day when the woman was getting ready to leave, "vy you go, my girl, eh? Stay hier bei me, und alle-ways you will me dat story ge-tellen, night und morgen, alle-ways. Hey? Yes?"

So it came about that the two were—we will say married, and for over a year, night und morgen Judy the story of the wonderful gold plate ge-told. Then a little child was born to her. The child has nothing to

*A short story
published in
The Wave of
October* 16, 1897.

do here, besides it died right away, no doubt its little body wasn't strong enough to hold in itself the blood of the Hebrew, the Spaniard and the Slav. It died. At the time of its birth Judy was out of her head, and continued so for upwards of two weeks. Then she came to herself and was as before.

Not quite. "Now ve vill have ut once eg-gain," said Knubel, "pe-gin, more dan one hoondurt bieces, und alle rad, rad gold."

"What's you talkin's about?" said Judy with a stare.

"Vy, about dat gold blate."

"I don't know about any gold plate, you must be crazy, Knubel. I don't know what you mean."

Nor did she. The trouble of her mind at the time of her little child's birth had cleared her muddy wits of all hallucinations. She remembered nothing of her wonderful story. But now it was Knubel whose red head was turned. Now it was Knubel who went about telling his friends of the wonderful gold service. But his mania was worse than Judy's.

"You've got ut, you've got ut zum-vairs, you she-swine," he would yell, clubbing Judy with a table leg. "Vair is ut, you've hidun ut. I know you've got ut. Vair is dose bunch-powl, vair is dose tsoop sboon?"

"How do I know?" Judy would shout, dodging his blows.

In fact how *did* she know?

Knubel went from bad to worse, ransacked the

A short story published in The Wave of October 16, 1897

house, pulled up the flooring, followed Judy when she went out as well as his game leg would allow, and peeped at her through keyholes when she was at home.

Knubel and Judy had a neighbor who was also an acquaintance, a Canadian woman who did their washing. Judy was sitting before the kitchen stove one morning when this woman came after the weekly wash. She was dead and must have been dead since the day before, for she was already cold. The Canadian woman touched her shoulder, and Judy's head rolled sideways and showed where Knubel had — well, she was dead.

Late in the day the officers found Knubel hiding about the old abandoned "Pavilion" that stands on top of the Hill. When arrested he had a sack with him full of rusty tin pans, plates and old tomato cans that he had gathered from the dump heaps.

"I got ut," said Knubel to himself, "I got ut, more dan a hoondurt pieces. I got ut at last."

The manufacture of cod liver oil from shark livers has languished of late, because of the hanging of Mister Knubel at San Quentin penitentiary.

*   *   *

And all this, if you please, because of a service of gold plate that never existed.

A Fantaisie Printaniere

A SHORT STORY FROM

The Wave *of November* 6, 1897.

The McTeagues and the Ryers lived at the disreputable end of Polk street, away down in the squalid neighborhood by the huge red drum of the gas works. The drum leaked, of course, and the nasty brassy foulness of the leak mingled with the odors of cooking from the ill-kept kitchens, and the reek of garbage in the vacant lots did not improve the locality.

McTeague had once been a dentist, and had had "parlors" up at the respectable end of the street. But after a while the license office discovered that he had no diploma; in fact, had never attended a college of any sort, and had forbidden him to practice. So McTeague had taken to drink.

Ryer, some years back, had been a sort of small stock-dealer on the outskirts of Butchertown, and had done fairly well until the Health Board reported him to the Supervisors because he had fattened his hogs on poultices obtained from the City and County Hospital. The result was a lamentable scandal, which finally drove him out of business. So Ryer had taken to drink.

Fantaisie Printaniere

The Ryers' home (or let us say, the house in which the Ryers ate and slept), adjoined the house in which the McTeagues ate and slept. You would have thought that this propinquity, joined with the coincidence of their common misfortunes—both victims of governmental persecution—would have insured a certain degree of friendship between the two men. But this was not so at all, a state of feud existed between Montague Ryer and Capulet McTeague. The feud had originated some year or so previous to the time of this tale, in the back room of Gerstle's "Wein Stube" on the corner opposite the drum. A discussion had arisen between the two men, both far gone in whiskey, as to the lines of longitude on the surface of the globe. Capulet claimed they were parallel throughout their whole extent—Montague maintained they converged at the poles. They discussed this question at length— first with heady words and vociferation, next with hurled pony glasses and uplifted chairs, and finally, after their ejection from the "Stube," with fists clenched till the knuckles whitened, crooked elbows, and the soles of heavy-shod boots. They arrived at no definite conclusion. Twice since then had they fought. Their original difference of opinion had been speedily forgotten. They fought now, they knew not why—merely for the sake of fighting. The quarrel between them came to be recognized by the "block" as part of the existing order of things, like the reek from the drum and the monthly visit of the rent-collector.

A short story published in The Wave *of November* 6, 189?

A short story published in The Wave *of November* 6, 1897.

Fantaisie Printaniere

Ryer had something the worst of it in these fights. He was a small, lean, pinkish creature, like a split carrot, his mouth a mere long slit beneath his nose. When he was angry his narrow eyes glistened like streaks of bitumen.

McTeague was a huge blonde giant, carrying his enormous fell of yellow hair, six feet and more above his ponderous, slow-moving feet. His hands, hard as wooden mallets, dangled from arms that suggested twisted cables. His jaw was that of the carnivora.

Both men thrashed their wives, McTeague on the days when he was drunk, which were many, Ryer on the days when he was sober, which were few. They went about it, each in his own peculiar fashion. Ryer found amusement in whipping Missis Ryer with a piece of rubber hose filled with gravel, or (his nature demanded variety of sensation), with a long, thin rawhide, which he kept hidden between the matresses. He never used fists or boots; such methods revolted him. "What! am I a drayman, am I a hod-carrier!" exclaimed Mister Ryer. When McTeague did not use the fist or the foot, he used the club. Refinement, such as characterized Ryer, was foreign to the ex-dentist. He struck out blindly, savagely, and with a colossal, clumsy force that often spent itself upon the air. The difference between the men could be seen in the different modes of punishment they affected. Ryer preferred the lash of the whip, McTeague the butt. Ryer was cruel, McTeague only brutal.

Fantaisie Printaniere

A short story published in The Wave *of* November 6, 189.

While common grievance had not made friends of the two men, mutual maltreatment had drawn their wives together, until no two women on the "block" were more intimate than Trina McTeague and Ryer's wife. They made long visits to each other in the morning in their wrappers and curl papers, talking for hours over a cuppa tea, served upon the ledge of the sink or a corner of the laundry table. During these visits they avoided speaking of their husbands, because, although the whole "block" knew of the occasional strained relations of their families, the two women feigned to keep the secret from each other. And this in the face of the fact that Missis Ryer would sometimes come over to see Trina with a thin welt across her neck, or Trina return the visit with a blackened eye or a split lip.

Once, however, only once, they broke in upon their reticence. Many things came of the infringement. Among others this fantaisie.

* * *

During that particular night three dandelions had bloomed in the vacant lot behind the gas works, the unwonted warmth of the last few days had brought back the familiar odor of the garbage heaps, an open car had appeared on the cross-town cable line and Bock beer was on draught at the "Wein Stube," and Polk Street knew that Spring was at hand.

About nine o'clock Trina McTeague appeared on

*A short story
published in
The Wave of
November 6, 1897.*

the back steps of her house, rolling her washtub before her, preparing to do her monthly washing in the open air on that fine morning. She and Ryer's wife usually observed this hated rite at the same time, calling shrilly to one another as their backs bent and straightened over the scrubbing-boards. But that morning Trina looked long for Missis Ryer and at last fell a-wondering.

The fact of the matter was that the night before Ryer had come home sober and had found occasion to coerce Missis Ryer with a trunk-strap. By a curious coincidence McTeague had come home drunk the same evening, and for two hours Trina had been hard put to it to dodge his enormous fists and his hurled boots. (Nor had she been invariably successful).

At that moment the ex-dentist was sleeping himself sober under the stairs in the front hall, and the whilom stock-dealer was drinking himself drunk in the "Wein Stube" across the street.

When eleven o'clock had struck and Missis Ryer had not appeared, Trina dried her smoking arms on her skirt, and, going through the hole in the back-yard fence, entered the kitchen of the Ryer's house and called. Missis Ryer came into the kitchen in a blue cotton wrapper and carpet slippers. Her hair was hanging down her back (it was not golden). Evidently she had just arisen.

"Ain't you goin' to wash this mornin,' Missis Ryer?" asked Trina McTeague.

A short story published in The Wave *of November 6, 189?*

"Good mornin,' Trina," said the other, adding doggedly, as she sat down hard in a broken chair: "I'm *sick* and *tired* a-washin' an' workin' for Ryer."

She drew up instinctively to the cold stove, and propped her chin upon her knuckles. The loose sleeve of the wrapper fell away from her forearm, and Trina saw the fresh marks of the trunk-strap. Evidently Ryer had not held that strap by the buckle-end.

This was the first time Missis Ryer had ever mentioned her husband to Trina.

"Hoh!" ejaculated Trina, speaking before she thought, "It ain't alwus such fun workin' for Mac, either."

There was a brief silence. Both the women remained for a moment looking vaguely out of the kitchen door, absorbed in thought, very curious, each wondering what next the other would say. The conversation, almost without their wishing it, had suddenly begun upon untried and interesting ground. Missis Ryer said:

"I'll make a cuppa tea."

She made the tea, slovening languidly about the dirty kitchen, her slippers clap-clapping under her bare heels. Then the two drew up to the washboard of the sink, drinking the tea from the saucers, wiping their lips slowly from time to time with the side of their hands. Each was waiting for the other to speak. Suddenly Missis Ryer broke out:

A short story published in The Wave *of November 6*, 1897.

"It's best not to fight him, or try to git away—hump your back and it's soonest over."

"You couldn't do that with Mac," answered Trina, shaking her head with decision; "if I didunt dodge, if I let um have his own way he'd sure kill me. Mac's that strong he could break me in two."

"Oh, *Ryer's* strong all-right-all-right," returned Missis Ryer, "an' then he's sober when he fights an' knows what he's about, an' that makes it worse. Look there what he did last night." She rolled up her sleeve and Trina glanced at the arm with the critical glance of a connoisseur.

"Hoh," she said scornfully, "that ain't a circumstance. I had a row with Mac last night meself, and this is what he did with his fist. Just his fist, mind you, and it only grazed me as it was." She slipped a discolored shoulder out of her calico gown. The two critically compared bruises. Missis Ryer was forced to admit that Trina's bruise was the worse. She was vexed and disappointed but rallied with:

"Yes, that's pirty bad, but I'll show you somethin' that'll open your eyes," and she thrust the biue wr ip-per down from the nape of the neck. "See that scar there," she said, "that's the kind of work Ryer can do when he puts his mind to it; got that nearly four months ago and it's sore yet."

"Ah, yes," said Trina loftily, "little scars, little flesh wounds like that! You never had any bones brokun.

*A short story
published in
The Wave of
November 6, 189*

Just look at that thumb," she went on proudly, "Mac did that with just a singul grip of his fist. I can't never bend it again."

Then the interminable discussion began.

"Luck at that, just look at *that*, will you."

"Ah, that ain't nothun. How about *that*, there's a lick for you."

"Why, Mac's the strongest man you ever *saw*."

"Ah-h, you make me tired, it ain't a strong man, always, that can hurt the most. It's the fellah that knows how and where to hit. It's a whip that hurts the most."

"But it's a club that does the most damage."

"Huh! wait till you get hit with a rubber hose filled with gravel."

"Why, Mac can knock me the length of the house with his left fist. He's done it plenty a' times."

Then they came to reminiscences.

"Why, one time when Mac came home from a picnic at Schuetzen Park, he picked me right up offun the ground with one hand and held me right up in the air like that, and let me have it with a kitchun chair. Huh! talk to *me* about Ryer's little whips, Ryer ain't a patch on my man. *You* don't know what a good thrashun *is*."

"I *don't*, hey, you can just listen to what I tell you, Trina McTeague, when I say that Ryer can lay all over your man. You jest ought a' been here one night when I sassed Ryer back, I tell you I'll never do *that* again. Why the worst lickin' Mister McTeague ever gave you was just little love taps to what I got. Besides I don't *believe* your man ever held you up with one hand and banged you like that with a chair, you wouldn't a' lived if he had."

"Oh, I ain't *lyun* to you," cried Trina, with shrill defiance getting to her feet. Missis Ryer rose likewise and clapped her arms akimbo.

"Why," she cried, "you just said as much yourself, that if you didn't dodge and get away he'd kill you."

"An' I'll say it again. I ain't gowun to eat my words for the best woman that ever wore shoes, an' you can chew on that, Missus Ryer. *I* tell you Mac's the hardust hittun husband a woman ever had."

"I just like to have you live here with Ryer a week or so, you'd soon find out who was the best man, an' — " here Missis Ryer came close to Trina and shouted the words in her face. "An' don't you sass me either, an talk about eatin' words, or I'll show you right here the kind a' whalin' Ryer's taught me."

"I guess Ryer, himself, knows who's the best man of the two, he or Mac," exclaimed Trina, loftily. "How about that last scrap o' theirs? If Mac got hold a' you once and gave you one lick, like the kind I get twenty of evury week, you wouldunt be as well off as your man was when Mac got through with um the time they fought last Washingtun's burthday, behind

A short story published in The Wave *of* November 6, 189·

the brick kiln. Why Mac could do for the whole three of us, you an' Ryer an' I, yes he could, with one hand."

"Ah, talk sense, will you," shouted Missis Ryer, as she moved the previous question. "Ain't Mister Mc-Teague drunk when he dresses you down, and don't it stand to reason that he *can't* give it to you as hard as Ryer gives it to me when he's *sober?*"

"Do you know anything about it anyways?" said Trina, excitedly, "I tell you he's a deal worse to me than Ryer ever *thought* of be-un to you. Ain't he twysut, *three* times as strong?"

"That's a lie," retorted Ryer's wife, vindicating her absent husband with astonishing vehemence.

"Don't you tell me I lie again," shouted Trina, her cheeks flaming, her chin thrust out.

"I guess I'll say what I please in my own kitchin, you dirty little drab," screamed the other. Their faces were by this time close together, neither would draw back an inch.

"No you won't, no you won't," panted Trina, "an' don't you dare call me a drab. Drab yourself; best go back to the pigs your man used to fatten on old poultices, go back to your sty, I guess it won't be any dirtier than this here kitchun."

"Git out of it then."

"Not till I get ready."

"An' I'll call you drab till I'm black in the face, drab,

A short story published in The Wave *of* November 6, 1897.

drab, dam nasty, dirty little drab. Get out uv my kitchin."

"Ah-h, let me see you put me out."

"Ah, dirty little drab."

"Ah, slattern, ah, pig feeder."

Suddenly they tore at each other like infuriated cats. A handful of black and gray hair came away from Missis Ryer's head. Fingernail marks, long red lines appeared on the curve of Trina's cheeks, very like McTeague's conception of the parallels upon a globe. Missis Ryer, hustling Trina toward the door, pushed her into the arms of McTeague himself. At the same time Ryer, warned of this war of wives, entered the kitchen from the front of the house. He had come over hastily from the "Wein Stube" and was half drunk. McTeague had partially slept off his intoxication and was about half sober.

"Here, here, here," cried the ex-dentist over his wife's shoulder, "you two women fightin', quit it, what the bloody Hell!"

"Scrappin'" shouted Ryer from the doorway, "Choke off, ol' woman, if there's any scrappin to be done, I'll do it meself."

"She called me a drab," gasped Trina, glaring at her enemy from under the protection of her gigantic husband.

"An' she said my kitchin wasn't a place for pigs to live in," retorted Missis Ryer, without taking her eyes from Trina.

A short story published in The Wave *of* November 6, 1897

The men had not yet looked at each other. They were unwilling to fight this morning, because each one of them was half drunk or half sober, (either way you choose to put it), and because Ryer preferred to fight when he had all his wits about him, while McTeague was never combative until he had lost *his* wits entirely.

"What started the row, whatcha been fightin' about?" demanded the ex-dentist.

"Yes, sure," put in Ryer, "whatcha been scrappin' about, what started the row?"

The women looked at each other, unable to answer. Then Trina began awkwardly:

"Well I—well—well—a—well she told me—she said —well, she run you down, Mac, an' I didunt figure on puttun up with it."

"She tried to make small of you, Ryer," said his wife, "an' I called her down, an'—that's all, she tried to make small of you."

"Hey? What'd she say?" demanded McTeague, "out with it."

"Well, *this* is what she said," exclaimed Trina suddenly. "She said Ryer could give her a worse dressing down than you ever gave me, an' I wouldn't stand it."

"Well," declared Missis Ryer, turning to her husband. "I ain't goin' to let every dirty little drab that comes along say—say—throw mud at my man, am I? I guess," added Missis Ryer, defiantly, facing Trina

A short story published in The Wave *of* November 6, 1897.

Fantaisie Printaniere

and the ex-dentist, "I guess Ryer can do what he likes in his own house. I ain't goin' to let any woman tell me that her man is better'n mine, in any way."

"An' that's what you two fought over," exclaimed the husbands in the same breath.

"Well, suppose we did," said Trina with defiance.

"I guess I can quarrel about what I like," observed Missis Ryer, sullenly.

For the first time since they had entered the room the eyes of the two men met, and for fully half a dozen seconds they looked squarely at each other. Then the corners of the slit under Ryer's nose began to twitch, and McTeague's huge jaws to widen to a grin in nutcracker fashion. Suddenly a roar of laughter shook him; he sank into a chair, rocking back and forth, smiting his knee with his palm. Ryer cackled shrilly, crying out between peals of laughter: "Well, if this ain't the greatest jolly I've struck yet."

"Fightin' over our fightin' *them*," bellowed McTeague.

"I've seen queer bugs in my time," gasped Ryer, "but the biggest curios yet are women, oh Lord, but this does beat the Dutch."

"Say, ain't this great, Ryer?"

"Mac, this does beat the carpet, sure."

"Look here old man, about them parallel lines, *I* say let's call it off. I ain't got no quarrel against *you*."

"That's a go, Mac, you're a good fellah, sure, put it there."

Fantaisie Printaniere

They shook hands upon their reconciliation, their breasts swelling with magnanimity. They felt that they liked one another hugely, and they slapped each other tremendous blows on the back, exclaiming at intervals "*put* it there," and gripping hands with a cordiality that was effusive beyond words. All at once Ryer had an inspiration.

"Say, Mac, come over to the Stube and have a drink on it."

"Well, I just guess I will," vociferated the ex-dentist.

Bewildered and raging at the unexpected reconciliation of their husbands, the two women had disappeared, Trina slamming the door of the kitchen with a parting cry of "pig feeder," which Missis Ryer immediately answered by thrusting her head out of a second story window and screaming at the top of her voice to the neighborhood in general, "dirty little drab."

Meanwhile the two men strode out of the house and across the street, their arms affectionately locked; the swing doors of the "Stube" flapped after them like a pair of silent wings.

*   *   *

That day settled the matter. Heretofore it had been the men who were enemies and their wives who were friends. Now the two men are fast friends, while the two women maintain perpetual feud. The "block" has come to recognize their quarrel as part of the

*A short story
published in
The Wave of
November 6, 1897.*

existing order of things, like the leak from the gas works and the collector's visits. Occasionally the women fight, and Missis Ryer, who is the larger and heavier, has something the best of it.

However, one particular custom common to both households remains unchanged—both men continue to thrash their wives in the old ratio—McTeague on the days when he is drunk (which are many), Ryer on the days when he is sober (which are few).

*A drawing by
Frank Norris from
the University of
California
Blue and Gold,
1894.*

Perverted Tales ❧

SIX PARODIES FROM

The Wave *of December* 24, 1897.

The discovery of California by the editors of the Big Four Magazines of the East has had the lamentable re-sult of crowding from their exalted places, heretofore so secure, a number of the world's most fascinating story-tellers. Their places have been filled from the ranks of that little army of youthful volunteers known as Les Jeunes. *As a lamentable result old idols have been over-thrown, old gods forgotten, and the children in the mar-ket place no longer dance to the tune of the old pipes. Where once the old favorite received a check, he now re-ceives a printed form with veiled reference to availability, guarded allusions to the plans of the editor—and his story. With the view to stemming the perverse tide of popular favor—whose ebb and flow are not reducible to any known law—and, if only for a moment, sounding again the old notes once so compelling, the editors of this paper have secured for publication a few of these rejected tales and here submit them to the public of the West. Their genuineness is as Caesar's wife, and if internal*

*A parody
published in
The Wave of
December 24, 1897.*

evidence were wanting, the opinions of experts in type-writing have been secured, which place their authenticity beyond fear and beyond reproach.

—Frank Norris, *Editor*

I. *The 'Ricksha that Happened*

BY R———D K———G

Ching-a-ring-a-ring ching-chow
Ho, dinkum darkey.—*The unedited diary of Bahla-mooca Tah.*

Jam yesterday and jam to-morrow
But never jam to-day.—*Native Proverb.*

"*Who's* all right? Rudyard! Who? *Rudyard!*"

—*Barrack-room ballad.*

There was a man once—but that's another story. Personally, I do not believe much of this story, however, you may have it for what it is worth, to me it was worth five thousand dollars per thousand words.

A friend of mine, who is a *jinricksha* down by Benares, told me this tale one hot evening outside the Tiddledtypore gate. In the telling of it he spat reflectively and often into the moat. *Chaprassi simpkin peg*, as Mrs. Hawkseye says.

Mulligatawney, who is a private soldier and who dines with me at table d'hote on Thursdays, and

A parody published in The Wave *of December 24, 189*

who shares my box at the opera, says the tale is cheap at a gallon and a half of beer.

"Pwhat nex!" exclaimed Mulligatawney, when he heard it, shifting his quid to the other side of his mouth (we were at table). "It's *jaddoo*, that's pwhat ut is. 'Tis flyin' in the face uv natoor to trifle with such brutil and licenshous soldiery as me and Orf-of-this an' Lear-eyed." Here he stole a silver spoon to hide his emotion. "*Choop*, sez oi to im," said Mulligatawney, filling himself another *jinricksha*, "*choop*, an' he chooped, like *ghairun* gone clane *dal-bat* an' *Kipiri* in hot weather. I waz only a recruity then. But I waz a corpril wanst. I was rejuced aftherwards, but I waz a corpril wanst," and he stared mournfully at the dying embers in the *jinricksha*.

We are a terrible bad lot out here in Indiana, but we can't help that. Here a man's whole duty is to lie *doggo* and not *ekka* more than once a week, and to pray for a war. Also he may keep a *jinricksha* in his stable if he can afford it. As that wonderful woman, Mrs. Hawkseye, says: "It's better to *bustee* in a *jampanni* than to have your *jinricksha puckarowed*." But that's her affair.

Stepterfetchit had just come out from *home*. Now when a man comes out from home, if he is not *jinrickshaed* at the pier landing, he generally does one of three things (*jampanni chorah simpkin bungalow*), either he dies with swiftness, which is bad, or lives

*A parody
published in
The Wave of
December 24, 1897.*

The 'Ricksha that Happened

with swiftness, which is worse, or marries, which is the worst of all. "A single man," says my friend Mulligatawney, "is an ornamint to the service." But as Lear-eyed observes, "when a mon is tewed wi' a lass he's *lokri* in a *bunder*, nothing but *dikh*," and he flung himself (seven foot four of British soldier), full length upon his *jinricksha*.

Stepterfetchit knew as much of Life (Life with a big L) as a weaning child, until I, who have seen everything worth seeing, and done everything worth doing, and have known everything worth knowing, from Indian magic to the cleaning of codfish, took him in hand. He began by contradicting his colonel, and went on from that to making love to Mrs. Hawks-eye (till that lady told him he was a *bungalow*, with no more *pukaree* than a *dacoit*), and wound up by drinking too much *jinricksha* at his club.

Now, when a man takes to the *jinricksha* he is very likely to end at the *shroff*. So I spoke to the Major. You may hit a *marumutta* over the head at the beginning of your acquaintance, but you must not soap the tail of a kitten that belongs to a *Ryotwary*, unless you are prepared to prove it on his front teeth. It takes some men a life time to find this out, but the knowledge is useful. *Sempkin peg, do re mi fa, ching-a-ring a-ring-ching-chow,* but that's another story. We arrived — the Major and I — at Stepterfetchit's dak-bungalow on a red hot evening, when the heat blan-

A parody published in The Wave *of December* 24, 18

keted the world like a hot towel round a swelled head. We nearly killed the *jinricksha* in getting there, but a mountain bred can *gawbry* more *jhil* than you would care to believe.

"Hark!" said the Major. We paused on the threshold and the silence of the Indian twilight gathered us in its hollow palms. We both heard a sound that came from Stepterfetchit's window. It was the ticking of an eight-day clock.

People write and talk lightly of blood running cold and of fear and all that sort of thing, but the real sensation is quite too terrible to be trifled with. As the Major and I heard the ticking of that eight-day clock, it is no lie to say that the *bhisti mussick* turned *shikary* in our *khitmatgar*. We were afraid. The Major entered the *bungalow* and I followed and *salaamed* the door behind me.

The *jinricksha* lay dead on the *charpoy* in Stepterfetchit's room. Stepterfetchit must have killed it hours before. "We came too late," groaned the Major. We made no attempt to keep from crying—I respected my self for that. But we gathered up the pieces of the *jinricksha* and sent them to Stepterfetchit's people at Home.

So now you know what I know of the Ricksha that never was.

Stepterfetchit is now a plate-layer somewhere down near Bareilly, on the line of the railroad, where the

A parody published in The Wave *of ember* 24, 1897.

Kharki water tanks that the Rajah of Bathtub built out of stolen government money, when the commissariat bullock train was *puckarowed* by Pathans, in the days of the old *budmash* Mahommud Dinare, and Mulligatawney is away annexing Burmah. When he heard of the affair he said:

"If a *punkah* is goin' to *ayah* niver loose your grip, but I waz a corpril wanst, I was rejuced afterwards," which is manifestly unfair.

Mrs. Hawkseye says that a "*jinricksha* in the hand gathers no moss"—but that's another story.

II. *The Green Stone of Unrest*

BY S——N CR——E

A Mere Boy stood on a pile of blue stones. His attitude was regardant. The day was seal brown. There was a vermillion valley containing a church. The church's steeple aspired strenuously in a direction tangent to the earth's center. A pale wind mentioned tremendous facts under its breath with certain effort at concealment to seven not-dwarfed poplars on an un-distant mauve hilltop.

The Mere Boy was a brilliant blue color. The effect of the scene was not un-kaleidoscopic.

After a certain appreciable duration of time the Mere Boy abandoned his regardant demeanor. The

*A parody
published in*
The Wave *of
December* 24, 18,

strenuously aspiring church steeple no longer pro-
jected itself upon his consciousness. He found means
to remove himself from the pile of blue stones. He set
his face valleyward. He proceeded.

The road was raw umber. There were in it wagon
ruts. There were in it pebbles, Naples yellow in color.
One was green. The Mere Boy allowed the idea of the
green pebble to nick itself into the sharp edge of the
disc of his Perception.

"Ah," he said, "a green pebble."

The rather pallid wind communicated another Incomprehensible Fact to the paranthine trees. It would
appear that the poplars understood.

"Ah," repeated the Mere Boy, "a Green Pebble."

"Sho-o," remarked the wind.

The Mere Boy moved appreciably forward. If there
were a thousand men in a procession and nine hundred and ninety-nine should suddenly expire, the one
man who was remnant would assume the responsibility of the procession.

The Mere Boy was an abbreviated procession.

The blue Mere Boy transported himself diagonally
athwart the larger landscape, printed in four colors,
like a poster.

On the uplands were chequered squares made by
fields, tilled and otherwise. Cloud-shadows moved
from square to square. It was as if the Sky and Earth
were playing a tremendous game of chess.

.1 parody published in The Wave of cember 24, 1897.

The Green Stone of Unrest

By and by the Mere Boy observed an Army of a Million Men. Certain cannon, like voluble but non-committal toads with hunched backs, fulminated vast hiccoughs at unimpassioned intervals. Their own invulnerableness was offensive.

An officer of blue serge waved a sword, like a picture in a school history. The non-committal toads pullulated with brief red pimples and swiftly relapsed to impassivity.

The line of the Army of a Million Men obnubilated itself in whiteness as a line of writing is blotted with a new blotter.

"Go teh blazes b'Jimminey," remarked the Mere Boy. "What yeh's shooting fur? They might be people in that field."

He was terrific in his denunciation.of such negligence. He debated the question of his ir-removability.

"If I'm goin' teh be shot," he observed; "If I'm goin teh be shot, b'Jimminey——"

*   *   *

A Thing lay in the little hollow.

The little hollow was green.

The Thing was pulpy white. Its eyes were white. It had blackish-yellow lips. It was beautifully spotted with red, like tomato stains on a rolled napkin.

The yellow sun was dropping on the green plain of the earth, like a twenty-dollar gold piece falling on the baize cloth of a gaming table.

*A parody
published in
The Wave of
December 24, 189*

The blue serge officer abruptly discovered the punctured Thing in the Hollow. He was struck with the ir-remediableness of the business.

"Gee," he murmured with interest. "Gee, it's a Mere Boy."

The Mere Boy had been struck with seventy-seven rifle bullets. Seventy had struck him in the chest, seven in the head. He bore close resemblance to the top of a pepper castor.

He was dead.

He was obsolete.

As the blue serge officer bent over him he became aware of a something in the Thing's hand.

It was a green pebble.

"Gee," exclaimed the blue serge officer. "A green pebble, gee."

The large Wind evolved a threnody with reference to the seven un-distant poplars.

III. *A Hero of Tomato Can*
BY B———E H———TE

Mr. Jack Oak-hearse calmly rose from the table and shot the bartender of Tomato Can, because of the objectionable color of his hair. Then Mr. Oak-hearse scratched a match on the sole of his victim's boot, lit a perfumed cigarette and strolled forth into

*A parody
published in
The Wave of
December 24, 1897.*

the street of the camp to enjoy the evening air. Mr. Oak-hearse's face was pale and impassive, and stamped with that indefinable hauteur that marks the professional gambler. Tomato Can knew him to be a cool, desperate man. The famous Colonel Blue-bottle was reported to have made the remark to Miss Honorine-Sainte-Claire, when that leader of society opened the Pink Assembly at Toad-in-the-Hole, on the other side of the Divide, that he, Colonel Blue-bottle, would be everlastingly "———— ————ed if he didn't believe that that ——— ————ed Oak-hearse would open a ————ed jack-pot on a pair of ————ed tens, ————ed if he didn't." To which Miss Ste.-Claire had responded:

"Fancy now."

On this occasion as Mr. Jack Oak-hearse stepped in the cool evening air of the Sierra's from out of the bar of the hotel of Tomato Can, he drew from his breast pocket a dainty manicure set and began to trim and polish his slender, almost feminine finger nails, that had been contaminated with the touch of the greasy cards. Thus occupied he betook himself leisurely down the one street of Tomato Can, languidly dodging an occasional revolver bullet, and stepping daintily over the few unburied corpses that bore mute testimony to the disputatious and controversial nature of the citizens of Tomato Can. He arrived at his hotel and entered his apartments, gently waving aside the half-breed Mexican who attempted to disembowel him on

A parody published in The Wave *of December* 24, 189

the threshold. The apartment was crudely furnished as befitted the rough and ready character of the town of Tomato Can. The Wilton carpet on the floor was stained with spilt Moet and Chandon. The full-length portrait of Mr. Oak-hearse by Carolus Duran was punctured with bullet marks, while the teak-wood escritoire, inlaid with buhl and jade, was encumbered with bowie knives, spurs and Mexican saddles.

Mr. Oak-hearse's valet brought him the London and Vienna papers. They had been ironed, and scented with orris root, and the sporting articles blue-penciled.

"Bill," said Mr. Oak-hearse, "Bill, I believe I told you to cut out all the offensive advertisements from my papers; I perceive, with some concern, that you have neglected it. Your punishment shall be that you will not brush my silk hat next Sunday morning."

The valet uttered an inarticulate cry and fell lifeless to the floor.

"It's better to stand pat on two pair than to try for a full hand," mused Mr. Oak-hearse, philosophically, and his long lashes drooped wearily over his cold steel-blue eyes, like velvet sheathing a poignard.

A little later the gambler entered the dining-room of the hotel in evening-dress, and wearing his cordon of the Legion of Honor. As he took his accustomed place at the table, he was suddenly aware of a lustrous pair of eyes that looked into his cold gray ones from the other side of the catsup bottle. Like all

*A parody
published in
The Wave of
December* 24, 1897.

heroes, Mr. Jack Oak-hearse was not insensible to feminine beauty. He bowed gallantly. The lady flushed. The waiter handed him the menu.

"I will have a caviar sandwich," affirmed the gambler with icy impassivity. The waiter next handed the menu to the lady, who likewise ordered a caviar sandwich.

"There is no more," returned the waiter. "The last one has just been ordered."

Mr. Oak-hearse started, and his pale face became even paler. A preoccupied air came upon him, and the lines of an iron determination settled upon his face. He rose, bowed to the lady, and calmly passed from the dining-room out into the street of the town and took his way toward a wooded gulch hard by.

When the waiter returned with the caviar sandwich he was informed that Mr. Oak-hearse would not dine that night. A triangular note on scented mauve paper was found at the office begging the lady to accept the sandwich from one who had loved not wisely but too many.

But next morning at the head of the gulch on one of the largest pine trees the searchers found an ace of spades (marked) pinned to the bark with a bowie knife. It bore the following, written in pencil with a firm hand:

*A parody
published in
The Wave of
December 24, 189-*

> Here lies the body
> of
> JOHN OAK-HEARSE,
> who was too much of a gentleman
> to play a Royal-flush
> against a
> Queen-full.

And so, pulseless and cold with a Derringer by his side and a bullet in his brain, though still calm as in life lay he who had been at once the pest and the pride of Tomato Can.

IV. *Van Bubble's Story*

BY R——D H——G D——S

Young Charding-Davis had been a little unhappy all day long because on that particular morning the valet of his head serving man had made a mistake in the matter of his master's trousers, and it was not until he was breakfasting at Delmonico's some hours later that young Charding-Davis woke to the painful consciousness that he was wearing his serving-man's pants which were made by an unfashionable New York tailor. Young Charding-Davis himself ran over to London in his steam yacht once or twice a week to be fitted, so that the consequences of his serving-

A parody
published in
The Wave of
December 24, 1897.

Van Bubble's Story

man's valet's mistake took away his appetite. The predicament troubled him so that he told the head cook about it, adding anxiously:

"What would you do about these trousers, Wallis?"

"I would keep 'em on, sir," said Wallis, touching his cap respectfully.

"That," said young Charding-Davis, with a sigh of relief, "is a good idea. Thank, you Wallis," Young Charding-Davis was so delighted at the novel suggestion that he tipped Wallis a little more generously than usual.

"Can you recommend a good investment for this?" inquired Wallis," as he counted out the tip.

"Make a bid for the Pacific railroads," suggested young Charding-Davis, "or 'arrive' at the Savoy Hotel."

That night he went to dinner at the house of the Girl He Knew, and in honor of the occasion and because he thought it would please the Girl He knew, young Charding-Davis put on a Yale sweater and football knickerbockers and the headdress of feathers he had captured from a Soudanese Arab while acting as war correspondent for an English syndicate. Besides this, he wore some of his decorations and toyed gracefully with a golf-stick. During the dinner, while young Charding-Davis was illustrating a new football trick he had just patented, with the aid of ten champagne bottles and the Girl's pet Skye terrier, a

*A parody
published in
The Wave of
December 24, 18.*

great and celebrated English diplomat leaned across the table over the center piece of orchids and live humming birds, and said:

"I say, Davis, tell us how you came by some of your decorations and orders. Most interesting and extraordinary, you know."

Young Charding-Davis tossed the Skye terrier into air, and batted it thoughtfully the length of the room with his golf-stick, after the manner of Heavyflinger of the Harvard baseball nine. Then he twirled the golf-stick in his fingers as a Zulu *induna* twirls his *assegai*—he had learned the trick while shooting elephant on the Zambesi river in South Africa. Then he smiled with becoming modesty as he glanced carelessly at the alarm-clock that hung around his neck, suspended by the blue ribbon of the order of the Pshaw of Persia.

"Really, they are mere trifles," he replied, easily. "I would not have worn them only my serving man insists it is good form. The Cham of Tartary gave me this," he continued, lightly touching a nickel-plated apple-pie that was pinned upon the sweater, "for leaving the country in twenty-four hours, and this chest protector was presented me by the French Legation in Kamschatka for protecting a chest—but we'll let that pass," he said, enveloping himself with a smile of charming ingenuousness. "*This* is the badge of the Band of Hope to which I belong. I got this pie-

*A parody
published in
The Wave of
December 24, 1897.*

plate from the Grand Mufti for conspicuous egoism in the absence of the enemy, and this Grand Army badge from a pawnbroker for four dollars. Then I have a few swimming medals for swimming across Whirlpool Rapids and a five-cent piece given me by Mr. Sage. I have several showcases full of other medals in my rooms. I'm thinking of giving an exhibition and reception, if I could get some pretty girls to receive with me. I've knocked about a bit, you know, and I pick them up here and there. I've crossed Africa two or three times, and I got up the late Greek war in order to make news for the New York papers, and I'm organizing an insurrection in South America for the benefit of a bankrupt rifle manufacturer who wants to dispose of some arms."

While Charding-Davis had been speaking young Van Bubbles, who was just out of the interior of Uganda, had been absent-mindedly drawing patterns in the tomato catsup he had spilled on the table-cloth.

"When I returned from Africa," he said, "this morning I had a curious experience." He fixed Charding-Davis with his glance for a moment, and then let it wander to a corner of the room and afterward drew it back and tied it to his chair leg. Charding-Davis grew a little pale, but he was too well bred to allow his feelings to overcome him. Young Van Bubbles continued:

A parody published in The Wave *of December* 24, 189

"I met an old valet of mine on Fifth avenue, who who has recently been engaged by the head serving man of one of New York's back-parlor heroes. He was wearing a pair of trousers which seemed to me strangely familiar, and when I spoke to him about the matter, broke down and confessed that he had caused his master's master to exchange trousers with him. You see the point of the story is," concluded young Van Bubbles, untying his glance, and allowing it to stray toward Charding-Davis, who drove it away with his golf-stick, "that the back-parlor hero wore his valet's trousers to-day."

There was a silence.

"What an extraordinary story," murmured the diplomat.

"Quite so," said the Girl Charding-Davis Knew.

"Of course," added Van Bubbles, "I took the trousers from him. Here they are," he continued, dropping them on the table. "You see they were no more use to him. I thought, perhaps—" and once more his glance crept stealthily toward young Charding-Davis —"*you* might suggest a way out of the difficulty." He handed the trousers to Charding-Davis, saying: "Keep them, they are a mere trifle, and they may be of some interest to you."

The Girl Charding-Davis Knew saw the point of Van Bubbles' story at once. Charding-Davis tried to catch her eye, but she refused to look at him, and said to her father.

.1 parody
published in
The Wave of
December 24. 1897.

"Why won't he go away; tell him to go away, please."

On the steps outside the house young Charding-Davis reflected what next he should do. He strolled slowly homeward, and, as he came into his rooms, his head serving man handed him two notes which had arrived in his absence. One was from the Most Beautiful Woman in New York offering him her hand and fortune; the other was written on the back of a ten thousand dollar check, and was from the Editor of of the Greatest Paper in the World begging him to accept the vacant throne of the Nyam-Nyam of Khooinooristan in the capacity of Special Correspondent.

"I wonder now," said young Charding-Davis, "which of these offers I shall accept."

V. *Ambrosia Beer*

BY A———E B———E

Sterling Hallmark was one of the most prominent and enthusiastic members of the Total Abstinence Union of San Francisco. His enthusiasm was not only of the passive description. He took a delight in aiding the police in their raids upon the unlicensed beer halls of the Barbary Coast. He helped them break whisky and brandy flasks, and he himself often opened the spigots of the beer kegs and let the foaming liquid run upon the sanded floor.

*A parody
published in
The Wave of
December* 24, 18

On the night of the thirtieth of February, 1868,
Sterling Hallmark led the police in a furious attack
upon the "Hole in the Wall," a notorious subteranean
dive in the vicinity of Jackson street. The battle was
short and decisive. The bartender and his assistants
were routed and the victorious assailants turned their
attention to the demolition of the unsavory resort.
Bottles were broken, brandy flasks smashed, the contents of the decanters emptied. In the midst of the
confusion Sterling Hallmark advanced with splendid
intrepidity towards a large keg, bearing the inscrip-
tion Ambrosia Beer, extra pale. He set his hand upon
the spigot.

But at that moment a terrific crash rent the air.
The frail building, in the cellar of which the "Hole in
the Wall" was situated, collapsed because it was necessary it should do so at that precise instant for the purposes of this tale. The crazy edifice fell with a loud
clatter and clouds of blinding dust.

When Sterling Hallmark recovered consciousness
he was not for the moment aware of what had happened. Then he realized that he was uninjured, but
that he was unmovably pinioned beneath a mass of
debris, and that something was weighing heavily upon
his chest. Looking up and around him he perceived in
the dim light a ring of metal protruding from a dark
object that lay upon his chest. As his senses adjusted
themselves to his environment he saw that the dark

96

*A parody
published in
The Wave of
December 24, 1897.*

object was the keg of Ambrosia Beer, and that the ring of metal was the mouth of the spigot. The mouth of the spigot was directly in the line of his lips and not two inches distant from them. The terrible question that now confronted Sterling Hallmark was this, Had he opened that spigot before the collapse of the building, was the keg full or empty? He now found that by great exertion he could move his right arm so that his fingers could touch and clasp the spigot. A horrible fear came upon Sterling Hallmark drops of cold perspiration bespangled his brow; he tried to cry out, but his voice failed him. His mouth was dry. A horrible thirst tortured him -- a thousand fiends seemed shouting to him to open the spigot, unseen hands tugged at *his* free hand. He raised this hand to cover his eyes from the sight, but as he withdrew it again it dropped upon his breast two inches nearer the fatal spigot. At length the strain became too great to be borne. Sterling Hallmark became desperate. He laughed aloud in almost insensate glee.

"Ha, Ha!" exclaimed Sterling Hallmark.

He reached up and grasped the spigot and turned it with all his strength.

*   *   *

An hour later when the rescue party with axes and hatchets found their way into the cellar of the "Hole in the Wall," the foremost of them hauled out Sterling Hallmark.

A parody published in The Wave *of December* 24, 18°

"Thash a' ri' girlsh," screamed the unfortunate man as his rescuers tried to keep him on his feet. "Thash a' ri,' I ne'r feelsh sho 'appy, az-I-do-t'-ni.' Les op'n n'er li'l' bol, girlsh." The patrol wagon was rung for, and the raving inebriate was conveyed to the City Hall. The ride in the open air, however, had the effect of sobering him. He realized that he, Sterling Hallmark, temperance leader, had been *drunk*. He also realized that he could not stand the disgrace that would now inevitably follow him through life. He drew his revolver, and ere the policeman who accompanied him could interfere, had sent a bullet crashing through his brain.

*   *   *

A few moments after the patrol wagon had departed one of the rescue party discovered the keg labelled Ambrosia Beer, that had been rolled from the breast of Sterling Hallmark. With a few well-directed blows of his ax, he smashed in the head of the keg, and thrust his hand down to the bottom, groping about.

The interior of the keg was full of dust and rusty nailheads.

"Empty for over a year," he exclaimed, in tones of bitter disappointment.

VI. *I Call on Lady Dotty*

FROM THE POLLY PARABLES

BY AN——Y H——PE

*A parody
published in*
The Wave *of
cember* 24, 1897.

Like most women, Lady Dotty is in love with me—
a little. Like most men, I am in love with Lady Dotty
—a great deal.

Last Thursday afternoon at five o'clock, as I was
strolling in St. James' Park (you may have remarked
that I always stroll—in St. James' Park—on Thursday afternoons) it occurred to me to call on Lady
Dotty. I forthwith presented myself at the house (it
is by Van Burgh).

After I had waited some five minutes in the drawing-room Lady Dotty appeared.

"But I am not at home," she said on the threshold.
"I am not at home, Mr. Carterer."

"Nor am I," I replied.

"And my husband is——"

"At home?"

"At his club."

"The brute," said I, "to leave you alone."

"There are others," she sighed, with half a glance
at me. I had not called in a fortnight.

"I have languished in self-imposed solitude," I murmured with some gallantry.

"Why have you not been to see me in so long?"

"My laundress——" I began.

*A parody
published in
The Wave of
December 24, 189*

"Your *laundress*, Mr. Carterer?"

"Refused to relent."

"You poor dear. Tea?"

"You are too kind," said I, with a bow.

Lady Dotty's maid, a delicious young creature named Negligee, appeared with the tray and smoking cups and vanished.

Lady Dotty handed me my cup.

"Sit down," she ordered.

There was but one chair in the room. I sat down.

Lady Dotty—also sat down.

"Clarence is a beast," she said.

"Most husbands are."

"Sometimes they are not."

"When?"

"When they are other women's husbands."

"Wives," I remarked, "of other men are no less so."

"Why can't other men's wives marry other women's husbands?" suggested Lady Dotty.

"The question is worthy of consideration," said I.

Negligee hurriedly entered at this point of our conversation.

"The husband of Madame," she exclaimed.

"Good heavens," said Lady Dotty.

I took my hat.

"Fly, Mr. Carterer," cried Lady Dotty.

"This way," murmured Negligee. "Follow me." She led me out into the dark hall, where the back stairs were.

I Call on Lady Dotty

A parody published in The Wave *of December* 24, 1897.

"It is rather dark, sir. You were best to give me your hand."

"And my heart," I answered.

Our hands clasped.

It was, as Negligee remarked, rather dark.

The charming creature's face was close to mine.

"Were you ever kissed?" said I, boldly.

"I don't know how to kiss," said Negligee.

"We might put our heads together and find out how," I suggested.

As I say, Negligee is a delicious young creature. But a man never knows the usefulness of his watch until he is without it—to say nothing of his scarfpin.

The Santa Cruz Venetian Carnival ❧

—AN ARTICLE REPRINTED

from The Wave of June 27, 1896.

You got off the train feeling vaguely intrusive. The ride from the city had, of course, been long and hot and very dusty. Perhaps you had been asleep for the last third of the way, and had awakened too suddenly to the consciousness of an indefinable sensation of grit and fine cinders, and the suspicion that your collar was limp and dirty. Then, before you were prepared for it, you were hustled from the train and out upon the platform of the station.

There was a glare of sunshine, and the air had a different taste that suggested the sea immediately. The platform was crowded, mostly with people from the hotels, come down to meet the train, girls in cool, white skirts and straw sailors, and young men in ducks and flannels, some of them carrying tennis rackets. It was quite a different world at once, and you felt as if things had been happening in it, and certain phases of life lived out, in which you had

. *In article
published in
The Wave of
June 27, 1896.*

neither part nor lot. You in your overcoat and gritty
business suit and black hat, were out of your element;
as yet you were not of that world where so many people knew each other and dressed in white clothes, and
you bundled yourself hurriedly into the corner of the
hotel 'bus before you should see anybody you knew.

It was a town of white and yellow. You did not
need to be told that these were the carnival colors.
They were everywhere. Sometimes they were in huge
paper festoons along the main street of the town,
sometimes in long strips of cambric wound about the
wheels of the hacks and express wagons, sometimes in
bows of satin ribbon on the whips of the private drags
and breaks. The two invariable color notes sounded,
as it were, the same pleasing monotone on every hand.
It was Thursday, June 18th. By then the carnival
was well under way. Already the Queen had been
crowned and the four days' and nights' reign of pleasure inaugurated amidst the moving of processions,
the clanging of brass bands, and the hissing of rockets.
Nothing could have been gayer than the sights and
the sounds of the town of Santa Cruz, as that hot
afternoon drew toward evening. The main street seen
in perspective was as a weaver's loom, the warp white
and yellow, the woof all manner of slow moving colors
—a web of them, a maze of them, intricate, change-
ful, very delicate. Overhead, from side to side, from
balcony to balcony, and from housetop to housetop,

An article published in The Wave *of June 27, 1896.*

stretched arches and festoons and garlands all of white and of yellow, one behind another, reaching further and further into the vista like the reflections of many mirrors, bewildering, almost dazzling. Below them, up and down through the streets, came and went and came again a vast throng of people weaving their way in two directions, detaching against the background of the carnival colors a dancing, irregular mass of tints and shades. Here and there was the momentary flash of a white skirt, again the lacquered flanks of a smart trap turned gleaming to the sun like a bit of metal, a feather of bright green shrubbery overhanging a gate stirred for a moment in the breeze very brave and gay, or a brilliant red parasol suddenly flashed into view, a violent, emphatic spot of color, disappearing again amidst the crowd like the quick extinguishing of a live coal.

And from this scene, from all this gaiety of shifting colors, rose a confused sound, a vast murmur of innumerable voices blending overhead into a strange hum, that certain unintelligible chord, prolonged, sustained, which is always thrown off from a concourse of people. It is the voice of an entire city speaking as something individual, having a life by itself, vast, vague, and not to be interpreted; while over this mysterious diapason, this bourdon of an unseen organ, played and rippled an infinite multitude of tiny staccato notes, every one joyous, the gay treble of a whole

*An article
published in
The Wave of
June 27, 1896.*

community amusing itself. Now it was a strain of
laughter, hushed as soon as heard, or the rattle of
stiffly starched skirts, or bits of conversation, an unfinished sentence, a detached word, a shrilly called
name, the momentary jangling of a brass band at a
street corner, or the rhythmic snarling of snare drums,
as a troop of militia or of marines passed down the
street with the creaking of leather belts and the ca-
denced shuffle of many feet.

And then little by little the heat of the afternoon
mingled into the cool of the evening, and the blue
shadows grew long and the maze of colors in the street
was overcast by the red glow of the sunset, harmoniz-
ing them all at last, turning white to pink and blue
to purple, and making of the predominant carnival
colors a lovely intermingling of rose and ruddy gold.
Then far down at the end of the street a single electric light flashed whitely out, intense, very piercing;
then another and then another. Then as rapidly as
the day darkened the little city set its constellation.
Whole groups and clusters and fine nebulae of tiny
electric bulbs suddenly bloomed out like the miracu-
lous blossoming of a Lilliputian garden of stars. The
city outlined itself, its streets, its squares, its larger
buildings in rows and chains and garlands of electricity, throwing off into the dark blue of the night a
fine silver haze. Then all at once from the direction
of the lagoon the first rocket hissed and rose, a quickly

lengthening stem of gold, suddenly bursting into a many-colored flower. A dozen more followed upon the moment; where one was twenty others followed; a rain of colored flames and sparks streamed down, there was no pause; again and again the rockets hissed and leaped and fell. The lagoon glowed like a brazier; the delicate silver electric mist that hung over the town was in that place rudely rent apart by the red haze of flame that hung there, fan-shaped, blood-red, distinct.

An article published in The Wave *of* *June* 27, 1896.

* * *

Later that same evening, about ten o'clock, Queen Josephine made her entry into the huge pavilion and gave the signal for the opening of the ball. The procession moved up the floor of the pavilion toward the throne (which looked less like a throne than like a photographer's settee). It advanced slowly, headed by a very little girl in a red dress, resolutely holding a tiny dummy trumpet of pasteboard to her lips. Then in two files came the ushers, *Louis Quatorze* style. They were all in white—white lace, white silk, white cotton stockings—and they moved deliberately over the white canvas that covered the floor against the background of white hangings with which the hall was decorated. However, their shoes were black—violently so; and nothing could have been more amusing than these scores of inky black objects moving back and forth amidst all this shimmer of white. The shoes

An article published in The Wave *of June 27, 1896.*

seemed enormous, distorted, grotesque; they attracted and fascinated the eye, and suggested the appearance of a migratory tribe of Brobdingnag black beetles crawling methodically over a wilderness of white sand. Close upon the ushers came the Queen, giving her hand to her prime minister, her long ermine-faced train carried by little pages. Pretty she certainly was. Tall she was not, nor imposing, nor majestic, even with her hair dressed high, but very charming and gracious nevertheless, impressing one with a sense of gaiety and gladness—a Queen *opéra comique*, a Queen suited to the occasion. The Prime Minister handed her down the hall. He wore an incongruous costume, a compound of the dress of various centuries—boots of one period, surcoat of another, a sword of the seventeenth century, and a hat of the early nineteenth; while his very *fin de siecle* E. & W. white collar showed starched and stiff at the throat of his surcoat. He was a prime minister *a travers les Ages*.

When Her Majesty was at length seated, the dancers formed a march and, led by Lieutenant-Governor Jeter, defiled before the Queen, making their reverences. Directly in front of the throne each couple bowed, some with exaggerated reverence coming to a halt, facing entirely around, the gentleman placing his hand upon his heart, the lady sinking to a deep courtesy, both very grave, and a little embarrassed;

An article published in The Wave *of June 27, 1896.*

others more occupied in getting a near sight of the Queen merely slacked their pace a bit, bending their bodies forward, but awkwardly keeping their heads in the air; others nodded familiarly as if old acquaintances, smiling into Josephine's face as though in acknowledgment of their mutual participation in a huge joke; and still others bowed carelessly, abstractedly, interrupting their conversation an instant and going quickly on, after the fashion of a preoccupied priest passing hurriedly in front of the altar of his church. The music was bad; there were enough square dances to give the ball something of a provincial tone, and the waltz time was too slow; yet the carnival spirit— which is, after all, the main thing—prevailed and brought about a sense of gaiety and unrestraint that made one forget all the little inconsistencies.

Friday afternoon brought out the floral pageant on the river. What with the sunshine and the blue water and bright colors of the floats and what with Roncovieri's band banging out Sousa's marches, it was all very gay, but nevertheless one felt a little disappointed. Something surely was lacking, it was hard to say exactly what. The tinsel on the boats *was* tinsel, defiantly, brutally so, and the cambric refused to parade as silk, and the tall lanterns in the Queen's barge wobbled. The program—that wonderful effort of rhetoric wherein the adjective "grand" occurs twenty-two times in four pages—announced a Battle,

An article published in The Wave *of June* 27, 1896.

a "grand" Battle of Flowers, but no battle was in evidence. True, I saw a little white boy with powdered hair, on the Holy Cross float, gravely throw a handful of withered corn-flowers at an elderly lady in a pink waist, in a rowboat maneuvered by a man in his shirt sleeves, and I saw the elderly lady try to throw them back with her left hand while she held her parasol with her right. The corn-flowers fell short, being too light to throw against the wind; they dropped into the water, and the elderly lady and the little white boy seriously watched them as they floated down stream. Neither of them smiled.

*   *   *

At about half-past eight Friday evening the rockets began to roar again from the direction of the lagoon. The evening fête was commencing.

On one side of the river were the Tribunes, two wings of them stretching out, half-moon fashion, from either side of the Governor's pavilion, banked high with row upon row of watching faces. Directly opposite was the Queen's pavilion, an immense canopy-like structure, flimsy enough, but brave and gay with tinsel and paint and bunting. Between the two pavilions was the waterway where the boats maneuvered. The "Bucentaur," the Queen's barge, came up the river slowly, gleaming with lanterns, a multitude of floats and barges and gondolas following. It drew up to the pavilion—the Queen's pavilion—and Josephine disembarked.

An article published in The Wave *of June 27, 1896.*

It was quite dark by now, and you began to feel the charm of the whole affair. Little by little the numbers of boats increased. Hundreds and hundreds of swinging lanterns wove a slow moving maze of trailing sparks and reflected themselves in the black water in long stillettoes with wavering golden blades; the rockets and roman candles hissed and roared without intermission; the enormous shafts of the searchlights, like sticks of gigantic fans, moved here and there, describing cartwheels of white light; the orchestra was playing again, not too loud. And then at last here under the night the carnival was in its proper element. The incongruities, the little, cheap makeshifts, so bare and bald in an afternoon's sun, disappeared, or took on a new significance; the tinsel was not tinsel any longer; the cambric and paper and paint grew rich and real; the Queen's canopy, the necklaces of electric bulbs, the thousands of heaving lights, the slow-moving "Bucentaur" all seemed part of a beautiful, illusive picture, impossible, fanciful, very charming, like a painting of Watteau, the *Embarquement Pour Cythére*, seen by night. More lights and lanterns came crowding in, a wheel of red fireworks covered the surface of the water with a myriad of red, writhing snakes. The illusion became perfect, the sense of reality, of solidity, dwindled. The black water, the black land, and the black sky merged into one vast, intangible shadow, hollow, infinitely deep. There was no longer

*An article
published in
The Wave of
June 27, 1896.*

the water there, nor the banks beyond, nor even the
reach of sky, but you looked out into an infinite,
empty space, sown with thousands of trembling lights,
across which moved dim, beautiful shapes, shallops
and curved prows and gondolas, and in the midst of
which floated a fairy palace, glittering, fragile, airy,
a thing of crystal and of gold, created miraculously,
like the passing whim of some compelling genie.

While the impression lasted it was not to be resisted;
it was charming, seductive—but it did not last. At
one o'clock the fête was over, the last rocket fired,
the last colored light burnt out in a puff of pungent
smoke, the last reveler gone. From the hill above the
lagoon on your way home you turned and looked
back and down. It was very late. The streets were
deserted, the city was asleep. There was nothing left
but the immensity of the night, and the low, red moon
canted over like a sinking galleon. The shams, the
paper lanterns, and the winking tinsel were all gone,
and you remembered the stars again.

And then, in that immense silence, when all the
shrill, staccato, trivial noises of the day were dumb,
you heard again the prolonged low hum that rose
from the city, even in its sleep, the voice of something
individual, living a huge, strange life apart, raising a
virile diapason of protest against shams and tinsels
and things transient in that other strange carnival,
that revel of masks and painted faces, the huge grim

joke that runs its fourscore years and ten. But that was not all.

There was another voice, that of the sea; mysterious, insistent, and there through the night, under the low, red moon, the two voices of the sea and of the city talked to each other in that unknown language of their own; and the two voices mingling together filled all the night with an immense and prolonged wave of sound, the bourdon of an unseen organ—the vast and minor note of Life.

An article published in The Wave *of June* 27, 1896.

A California Jubilee

AN ARTICLE REPRINTED

from The Wave of July 11, 1896.

Tuesday was the bright particular day of the Monterey celebration; the ceremonies appropriate to the occasion were performed under a cloudless sky and in the midst of enormous crowds. It would have been impossible to have recognized the old town of Monterey during the days of the celebration. Its sidewalks were jammed with a slow moving throng, its houses were festooned, its streets garlanded. At every turning and in every direction the eye was almost dazzled by the stretch of blinding tricolor that wound spirally around everything that could be called a pole. The main street of the town suggested the Midway Plaisance; every shop seemed a bazaar, while on either edge of the sidewalk sprang up a magic mushroom growth of booths and tents; peanut men, popcorn men, tamale and fruit men, chanted a minor chorus without a moment's interruption. There were public phonographs, merry-go-rounds, tintype photographers, nickel-in-the-slot machines by the scores. Even the calling-card writer with his famous bird of paradise drawn in lovely curves and sweeps was on hand

An article published in The Wave *of July 11, 1896.*

and found occasion to turn the nimble penny. All sorts and conditions of men paraded the streets, Mexican war veterans, Grand Army men, militia, marines cowboys, men in flannels and ducks from Del Monte, Mexicans and Spaniards in sugar-loaved sombreros, and touring Englishmen in tweeds and pith-helmets, very puzzled to know what was going forward.

On Tuesday morning occurred the laying of the foundation stone of the Sloat monument. It was deadly hot. Up the hill from all sides, across the potato and cabbage patches, over the slippery dry and yellow grass trudged and scrambled the assembling crowd. Many of them had come in dusty, rattling buggies from the surrounding country. The old rattle-traps stood about by the dozen, the aged horse, unhaltered, tossing at his nose-bag, the lunch under the back seat covered with a plaid shawl or a red table-cloth, the old setter-dog asleep in the shadow of the lowered top.

The crowd was densely packed around the crane that held the corner stone. It was of country folk for the most part, to whom that day was a veritable event, something to be taken very seriously and to be talked about for the next five days. There, under the broiling sun, they stood, wedged-in, perspiring, very grave. A cordon of the Masons of the town made room about the unfinished monument. They wore white cotton gloves that showed the wrist below the cuff, red, fat

An article published in The Wave of July 11, 1896.

and beaded with perspiration. In their left hands they carried long wands with all the gravity of lictors, while about their stomachs were absurdly tied their Masonic aprons like flabby mail pouches, lamentably incongruous with their frock coats and carefully polished silk hats. The orations began. There were references to "Old Glory," "gratitude of the American people," "fitting tributes." The crowd listened with attention, carefully applauded the most distant allusion to freedom. Then, at last, with a great rattle of chains and a groaning of strained timbers, the huge stone was lowered into place. The crowd broke up, the women gathering up the hot and fretting bundles of infancy, the men tramping back to the buggies stolidly, thrusting out their chins in approbation. They had the air of men who have accomplished a duty, and they put on their coats again complacently.

That afternoon the Flag was raised. You had an undoubted thrill at the precise moment of the raising when the vast flag grew into the air like the slow flight of some immense, beautiful bird, and the salutes began to speak from the Philadelphia and Monadnock. It was fine and exhilarating, and worth while, and it made one forget for a moment some few of the drawbacks of the business—such, for instance, as the splendid new coat of whitewash that in honor of the occasion had been applied to the old Custom House.

Towards 2 o'clock the cortege arrived in front of

An article published in The Wave *of July* 11, 1896.

this ancient building, preceded by a train of artillery and escorted by the Philadelphia marines. The main features of the procession were the two floats, one carrying the big blonde girl who represented the Goddess of Liberty, and the other the allegorical group of California made up of three very pretty girls in smart white frocks. Following these were the 200 Mexican War veterans, very old fellows, walking uncertainly, dazed for the most part, looking bewilderedly about them with wide eyes, and, after these, the little red-white-and-blue girls who sat in the grand stand in appropriate rows and made the "Living Flag." They were excited and chattering, and suggested a troupe of little trained animals on exhibition. Then after the members of the procession had been disposed about the grand stand, more speeches were delivered, by the Mayor of Monterey, by Congressman McLachlan, the President of the day; then came a prayer by a naval chaplain, a reading of Sloat's proclamation by his grandson, a "vocal selection" and a chorus by the little red-white-and-blue girls and finally the reading of an address by E. A. Sherman, the Commander of the day.

Ah, that Commander of the day, what a figure he was with his bristling gray beard, his huge campaign hat and his fearful array of medals. Never was there a man so weighted down with the responsibility of his position. He directed, he organized, he presided, he

An article published in The Wave of July 11, 1896.

exhorted and commanded, he shouted and roared like an unleashed lion, the fate of nations rested upon his shoulders, the destinies of a whole race trembled upon the utterance of his tongue. From dawn to dewy eve Mister Sherman played a part, a heroic, gold-laced part, and he played it well. He was a procession, a whole brigade, all in himself; he assumed commanding attitudes—Grant reviewing his army, Washington delivering his inaugural address, Wellington at Waterloo. He posed for the gallery. He was a series of living pictures all the more delightful because he succeeded in deceiving even himself.

Then at last out of all this fanfaronade, with the suddenness and unexpectedness of a rising rocket came the great flag, raised there by the same hands that raised it on that same staff, over that same old building so many years ago. There was a great cheer, genuine, true, with the right ring in it. And you were not ashamed to cheer yourself, and as the marines and officers saluted and as the great guns aboard the two war ships crashed and shouted, you felt a touch of the real thing itself, a touch of that fine enthusiasm which Sloat and his men must have felt when that flag strained at its halyards there on that desolate shore a whole half-century ago, when, for once at least, an English scheme of land-grabbing was balked and a strip of country far larger than the whole kingdom of Great Britain added to the Union.

It was fine and strong. Why not be glad in the great barred banner—patriotism was, after all, something better than rhetoric and firecrackers. You felt glad that you were there, that, for all its failings, the ceremony of the Flag Raising stood for something that was good. It was worth while after all.

An article published in The Wave *of* *July* 11, 1896.

Hunting Human &

Game AN ARTICLE FROM

𝕿𝖍𝖊 𝖂𝖆𝖛𝖊 *of January* 23, 1897.

On the 21st of November in the year 1896 there appeared in one of the newspapers of Sydney, Australia, an advertisement to the effect that one Frank Butler —mining prospector, was in search of a partner with whom to engage in a certain mining venture. It was stipulated that applicants should possess at least ten pounds and come well recommended.

Captain Lee Weller answered the advertisement and accompanied Butler to the Blue Mountains mining region, in what is known as the Glenbrook district. There Butler shot him in the back of the head and buried the body in such a way that a stream of trickling water would help in its decomposition. But Captain Weller had friends; he was missed; a search was made and it was not long before the detectives discovered the grave and identified the remains.

Meanwhile, news had been brought to the Australian police that another man named Preston had gone into the mountains and never returned. Next the body of this Preston was discovered. Then it was

*An article
published in
The Wave of
January 23, 189*

found that another man had disappeared under the same circumstances as those surrounding the vanishing of Weller. Then another and another, and still another. The news of these disappearances ran from end to end of Australia, and the whole police system of the country was brought to bear upon the case. Finally it was found that a man named Lee Weller had applied to the Sailor's Home at Newcastle for a berth on a ship. Seven days later this Lee Weller shipped out of Newcastle before the mast on the British tramp ship Swanhilda, bound for San Francisco in coal. This was all the detectives wanted to know. The man calling himself Weller was Butler beyond any doubt, suddenly grown suspicious and resolved upon a bolt. Butler's photograph was identified at once by the Superintendent of the Sailor's Home as the supposed Lee Weller. It was out of the question to overhaul Butler now, but two Australian detectives, McHattie and Conroy, took passage on a steamer for San Francisco, where they arrived some three weeks ago. They outstripped Butler and are now waiting for him to catch up with them. That is the story in brief of this extraordinary criminal who, Mr. McHattie says, has killed—no, assassinated is the word—fourteen men.

I saw the "death watch" the other day—the watch for the tramp collier ship Swanhilda—that is being maintained at Meiggs' wharf by seven men, whose

*An article
published in*
The Wave *of*
January 23, 1897.

business it is to hunt criminals down. There is but little of that secrecy and dark mystery about this famous "death watch" that sensational story-writers would have you believe. The detectives live upstairs in a little two-story house at the end of Meiggs' wharf, close to the customs offices. I had imagined that I would be met at the door with all sorts of difficulties, that permits and passes would be demanded and explanations and the like; that the detectives would be austere and distant and preoccupied, preoccupied as men are who are watching for a sign or listening for a signal. Nothing of the sort. I tramped in at the open door and up the stairs to the room and sat me down on Mr. McHattie's bed—it's a lounge, but it does for a bed—as unchallenged as if the place had been my own; nor was I armed with so much as a letter of introduction. I was not even asked to show a business card.

The room is a little room, whose front windows give out upon the bay and the Golden Gate. Not a row-boat could pass the Gate without being noted from this vantage point. There were four beds made up on the floor of the room, and Conroy was dozing in one, pretending to read "Phra the Phoenician," the whiles. The other detectives sat about a gas stove, smoking. They were for the most part big, burly men, with red faces, very jovial and not at all like the sleuths you expected to see. They are, however, heavily mus-

*An article
published in
The Wave of
January* 23, '18

cled fellows, with the exception of Conroy, who singularly enough is slighter than any of them, though a
trained athlete. I remember that the room was warm.
That there were pictures of barks and brigs about
the walls, that a pair of handcuffs were in a glass dish
on the top of a dresser, and that, lying in a cubby
hole of a desk, was Detective Egan's revolver in a
very worn case. The detectives impressed one as positively jolly. They told me many funny yarns about
the crowd of visitors on the wharf, of the "Branch
office of the Chronicle," a room ten feet square, just
back of the Customs building, and once when "The
Examiner" reporter cried out that a girl was waving
a handkerchief from a window on the hill back of the
wharf, they made a rush for the rear window of the
room, crowding about it like so many boys.

And at that very moment somewhere out there beyond the Farallones a certain great four-masted ship,
58 days out of Newcastle, was rolling and lifting on
the swell of the Pacific, drawing nearer to these men
with every puff of the snoring trades. Some time within
the next few days the signal from the Merchants' Exchange will be rung in that room, there on Meiggs'
wharf the signal which some of these men have come
around half of the world to hear. It will be rung on
the telephone bell, and it may come at each instant—
it may be ringing now as I write these lines, or now
as you read them. It may come in the morning, or

*An article
published in
The Wave of
January* 23, 1897.

while the "watch" is at supper, or in the very dead of night, or the early dawn. May I be there to hear it and to see as well. The scene cannot be otherwise than dramatic—melodramatic even. I want to hear that exclamation "Here she is" that some one is bound to utter. I want to see Egan reach for the revolver in the worn leather case, and Conroy take the handcuffs from the glass dish. I want to see the sudden rousing of these seven men, these same men who waved their hands to the girl in the window, and I want to hear the clatter of those seven pairs of boots going down the stair and out upon the wharf. I fancy there will not be much talking.

The Bombardment

AN ARTICLE REPRINTED

from The Wave of April 3, 1897.

I arrived in Crete the day after the bombardment. Many things had happened, but everything was then over. I cursed the quarantine officers who had delayed the steamer, and set about collecting local color, for there was plenty of that left around—thank Heaven!

I salted down all my information and filled a small note book with the data. I made a bluff at a few sketches and betook myself home. I was no reporter, so it didn't much matter. I was only indulging in a little three months' fling at the Orient, and I wasn't much disappointed at not catching snap shots of the excitement.

I wrote it all up on the way across the Atlantic, and had it in shape by the time I reached New York—about three thousand words that everybody said was "good stuff." It seemed to me that it was "timely," too, and I sent it off with postage enclosed to *Harper's Monthly*. It came back, of course—they always do—and I had made a try at the *Century* and several of the half-tone monthlies, but it was always marked "down." I had some good letters introducing me to the editors, and I got personal replies, but by the time I reached San Francisco I gave the thing up and put it away.

An article published in The Wave of · *April 3, 1897.*

After I had been home a month or so, a friend invited me to a meeting of the "Chit-Chat" Club, and I was very much impressed. There was more intellectuality to the square inch of waistcoat than I had thought possible in this town. It was rather heavy, but it was solid—there were bankers with libraries and merchants with microscopes, who encourage "local art"; they affected social questions, and had a blown-in-the-bottle culture that was almost convincing. I had to stand on tiptoe (so to speak) in order to keep up with the level of their statistics, but I must say I was flattered when they asked me to read my paper on the "Bombardment" at the next meeting.

There were many questions I couldn't answer after that reading. Good Heavens! how should I know about the armament of the fleet of the Powers? They had a long discussion over the embroglio, in which I was left carefully out of the question, but they gave me a vote of thanks, and would have had the essay printed if I hadn't objected.

The next day I met Leggett. Leggett is the wit of the "6:30" Club, and he wanted me to come around, for the 6:30's were to dine that night. So I went. The men there were all younger than the Chit-Chats, whom they guyed audibly. They were all coming men —men who hoped soon to arrive—and it seemed to be the club's office to corner the budding talent of the town. There was a bunch of *Overland Monthly*

An article published in The Wave *of April* 3, 1897.

men who should have been in the Chit-Chat by this time, but still clung to the youngsters.

I was unanimously elected a member of the 6:30—the Lord knows why, perhaps because my name begins with "S" and they had got down to the "Rs" in the round of papers delivered each month. At any rate, I found I had to read something of my own at the next meeting. I didn't say anything about the Chit-Chat paper, but I had no time to do anything else, so I read the "Bombardment." They are rare wags at the 6:30. Telegraph boys came in with messages from hypothetical publishers at each course bidding for the manuscript (they eat a 75-cent dinner at the Poodle Dog), and they chaffed me every time I tried to put in a flourish that wasn't written down. Each man, in his order, gave his critique of the essay, and it was very generously damned. I went home and threw the manuscript in the trunk and thought it was played out. Not much.

Next week Wednesday I received a note in a slashing chirography from a lady who "really must insist upon my reading the charming paper that I had recently written before the Century Club, as they had set the subject for that week 'Athens and the Athenians'—and they must have it." I wrote her there was nothing about Athens in the article, and that I was engaged for Thursday. She telephoned me that "Crete would do perfectly, and I simply must come because the arrangements had been made."

An article published in The Wave *of April* 3, 1897.

So I stood up and read my paper—I was the only man in the room, and they lorgnetted me without mercy. I was told afterwards that the lady who had invited me had been blackballed four times, and when she had finally been elected she had sworn to get even with the club. But they stood it breathlessly, and the next week they had as bad a paper on "Household Art."

I had begun to think myself quite a litterateur by this time—everybody spoke of my "Bombardment," and I couldn't go to a mauve tea without being introduced as its author.

I read it next at the Geographical Society, sandwiched in between Dr. Harkness' "Paleolithic Theories" and David Starr Jordan on "Retrograde Movements of the Common Arab." I was the only one who didn't have lantern-slides, and the audience of six women and two men filled the Academy of Sciences with their yawns.

Well, I read the "Bombardment" at the Sketch Club next, at the earnest solicitation of the President, who instructed the audience when to applaud—they had the shades down and lighted the studio with brass candlesticks and marigolds. The manuscript was about worn out by this time, but I knew the thing by heart, and fully believed I had been in Canea at the time of the shelling. One more reading, and I felt I should have met every woman worth knowing in town. So when the Fortnightly sent for me I had

An article published in The Wave *of* April 3, 1897.

already acquired a manner, and I did the impressing myself, instead of submitting to the operation. There was a wild striving for intellectuality written on the faces of the Fortnightlies. All of them had written papers themselves—papers crammed with measurements and distances that took hours to look up. It was an off day on account of a protracted Maeterlinck recitation the week before, and all the Vassar girls were absent. There was a rarefied lemonade with wafers passed around after I had performed, and the talk relapsed into the discussion of engagements. An engagement in the Fortnightly is an event, for wildly intellectual girls don't marry till quite late in life.

I read the paper at Miss Head's school next, and my fame was confided to the tender mercies of a coming generation. I read it in the assembly hall at Berkeley. I read it in the private salon of Mrs. Beebe, a woman of gush and giggle, who entertains local celebrities on Sunday afternoons.

I am growing old now, but I am still the author of the "Bombardment." I have made my name and I intend to keep it. I have been offered a six months' subscription to the *Overland* for its publication in that magazine, but I know a good thing when I have it, and there are yet clubs in town. For we have begun the revival of culture in San Francisco and have already promised to become a "centre."

"JULIAN STURGIS"

At Home from Eight to Twelve & AN ARTICLE

from **The Wave** *of January* 1, 1898.

Every window of the house was lighted. The front
door was opened for the guest before he could ring
and he passed up the stairs, catching a glimpse of the
parlors through the portieres of the doors. At the
turn of the stairs the second girl in a white lawn cap
directed them to the gentlemen's dressing-room, which
was the room of the son of the house. About a dozen
men were there already, some rolling up their overcoats into balls and stowing them with their canes
in the corners of the room, others laughing and smoking together, and still others who were either brush-
ing their hair before the mirrors, or sitting on the bed
in their stocking feet breathing upon their patent
leathers, warming them before putting them on. There
were one or two who knew no one and who stood
about unhappily, twisting the tissue paper from the
the buttons of their new gloves, looking stupidly at
the pictures on the walls of the room. Occasionally
one of the gentlemen would step to the door, looking
out in the hall to know if the ladies whom he was es-

An article
published in
The Wave *of*
January 1, 1898.

corting were yet come out of their dressing-room, ready to go down.

The house was filling up rapidly, one heard the deadened roll of wheels in the street outside, the banging of carriage doors, and an incessant rustle of stiff skirts ascending the stairs. From the ladies' dressing-room came an increasing soprano chatter, while downstairs the orchestra around the piano in the back parlor began to snarl and whine louder and louder. About the halls and stairs one caught brief glimpses of white and blue opera cloaks edged with swansdown, alternating with the gleam of a starched shirt bosom and the glint of a highly polished silk hat. Odors of sachet and violets came and went elusively, or mingled with those of the roses and pinks. An air of gaiety and excitement began to spread throughout the whole house.

But an hour later the dance was in full swing. Almost every number was a waltz or a two-step, the music being the topical songs and popular airs of the day set to dance music. Some of the couples waltzed fast whirling around the rooms, bearing around corners with a swirl and swing of silk skirts, the girl's face flushed and perspiring, her eyes half closed, her bare white throat warm, moist and alternately swelling and contracting with her slow breathing. On certain of these girls the dancing produced a peculiar effect. The continued motion, the whirl of the lights,

At Home from Eight to Twelve

An article published in The Wave *of January 1, 1898.* /

the heat of the room, the heavy perfume of the flowers, the cadence of the music, even the physical fatigue reacted in some strange way upon their oversensitive feminine nerves, the monotony of repeated sensation producing some sort of mildly hypnotic effect, a morbid hysterical pleasure, the more exquisite because mixed with pain. These were the girls whom one heard declaring that they could dance all night, the girls who could dance until they dropped.

About the doors and hallways stood the unhappy gentlemen who knew no one, watching the others dance, feigning to be amused. Some of them, however, had ascended to the dressing-room and began to strike up an acquaintance with each other, smoking incessantly, discussing business, politics and even religion.

In the ladies' dressing-room two of the maids were holding a long conversation in low tones, their heads together. Evidently it was concerning something dreadful. They continually exclaimed "Oh" and "Ah," suddenly sitting back from each other, shaking their heads, biting their nether lips. Out in the hall on the top floor the servants in their best clothes leant over the balustrade nudging each other, talking in hoarse whispers or pointing with thick fingers, swollen with dishwater. All up and down the stairs were the couples who were sitting out the dance, some of them even upon the circular sofa in the hall of the first landing.

*An article
published in
The Wave of
January* 1, 1898.

Supper was served in the huge billiard room in the basement, and was eaten in a storm of gaiety. The same parties and "sets" tried to get together at the same tables.

One ate oysters *a la poulette*, terrapin, salads and croquettes, the wines were Sauternes and Champagnes. With the nuts and dessert, the caps came on and in a few minutes were cracking and snapping all over the room.

Six of the unfortunates who knew no one, but who had managed, through a common affliction, to become acquainted with each other, gathered at a separate table. They levied a twenty-five cent assessment upon each other and tipped the waiter a dollar and a half; this one accordingly brought them a bottle of Champagne apiece, in which they found consolation for all the *ennui* of the evening.

After supper the dancing began again. The little stiffness and constraint of the earlier part of the evening was gone; by this time nearly everybody, except the unfortunates, knew everybody else. The good dinner and the Champagne had put them all into an excellent humor, and they all commenced to be very jolly. They began a Virginia reel still wearing the Magician's caps and Phrygian bonnets of tissue paper.

Toward one o'clock there was a general movement. The ladies of the house were inquired for, and the blue and white opera cloaks, reappeared descending the

An article published in The Wave *of January* 1, 1898.

At Home from Eight to Twelve

stairs, disturbing the couples who were seated there. The banging of carriage doors and the rumble of wheels recommenced in the street. The musicians played a little longer. As the party thinned out, there was greater dance room and a consequent greater pleasure in dancing, and these last dances at the end of the evening were enjoyed more than all the others. But ten minutes later the function was breaking up fast. Suddenly the musicians played "Home, Sweet Home." Those still dancing uttered an exclamation of regret, but continued waltzing to this air the same as ever. Some even began to dance again in their overcoats and opera-wraps. Then at last the tired musicians stopped and reached for the cases of their instruments, and the remaining guests, seized with a sudden panic lest they should be the last to leave, fled to the dressing-rooms. These were in the greatest confusion, everyone was in a hurry. In the gentlemen's dressing-room there was a great putting on of coats and mufflers and a searching for misplaced gloves, hats and canes. A bass hum of talk rose in the air, bits and ends of conversation being passed back and forth across the room. "*You* haven't seen my hat have you, Jimmy?" "Did you meet that girl I was telling you about?" "Hello, old man; have a good time to-night?" "Lost your hat?" "No, *I* haven't seen it." "Yes, about half-past ten." "Well, I told him that myself." "Ah, you bet, it's the man that rustles

An article published in The Wave *of* *January* 1, 1898.

that gets there." "Come around about four, then." "What's the matter with coming home in *our* carriage?" At the doors of the dressing-rooms the ladies joined their escorts, and a great crowd formed in the hall, swarming down the stairs and out upon the front steps. As the first groups reached the open air there was a great cry, "Why, it's pouring rain." This was taken up and repeated, and carried all the way back into the house. There were exclamations of dismay and annoyance. "Why, it's raining right *down*." "What *shall* we do?" Tempers were lost, brothers and sisters quarreling with each other over the question of umbrellas.

In a short time all the guests were gone, except the one young lady whose maid and carriage had somehow not been sent. The son of the hostess took this one home in a hired hack. The hostess and her daughter sat down to rest for a moment in the empty parlors. The canvass-covered floors were littered with leaves of smilax and la France roses, with bits of ribbon, ends of lace and discarded Phrygian bonnets of tissue paper. The butler and the second girl were already turning down the gas in the other rooms.

Cosmopolitan San Francisco

AN ARTICLE REPRINTED

from The Wave *of Dec.* 24, 1897.

In a way San Francisco is not a city—or rather let us say, it is not *one* city. It is several cities. Make the circuit of these several cities and by the time you have come to the severalth you may say with some considerable degree of truth; "I have seen Peking and have walked the streets of Mexico, have looked on the life of Madrid, have rubbed elbows with Naples and Genoa, glanced in at Yokohama, even—though more remotely, perhaps—have known Paris and Berlin.

What is true of San Francisco is true of California. As yet we, out here, on the fringe of the continent, with the ocean before and the desert behind us, are not a people, we are peoples—agglomerate rather than conglomerate. All up and down the coast from Mexico to Oregon are scattered "little" Italys, "little" Spains, "little" Chinas, and even "little" Russias—settlements, colonies, tiny groups of nationalities flung off from the parent stock, but holding tightly to them-

selves, unwilling to mix and forever harking back to
their native lands.

*An article
published in
The Wave of
December 24, 18..*

But it is a rather curious fact that, though the
Anglo-Saxons are the great mining peoples, and though
the confusion of nations in California is due almost
solely to the rush for gold, it is, nevertheless, the *Latin*
and not the *German* races that are in greater evidence
among us. Ireland has stopped in New York and Boston and on the Atlantic seaboard, and it is hard to
coax Germany across the Mississippi.

It is not hard to understand why Mexico should be
here, and Spain is readily accounted for. But why
the Chinaman? There are two almost iron-clad ten-
dencies *against* his presence. First, the tendency in
obedience to which nations move from East to West,
and second, the bred-in-the-bone tendency of the
Chinaman to stay where he is put, to live and labor and
die within a ten mile radius of his birthplace. No
nation in the world is more tenacious of the hearth-
stone than the Mongolian. Yet, of all the foreign colonies in California and San Francisco, none are larger
or more distinct than the Chinese. A curious state of
affairs when you think about it, and for which you
can offer no explanation.

By way of parenthesis—and though they are only
apparent by traces of former occupation—think for a
moment how narrowly California escaped an influx
of the Russians. Somewhere in the interior of Big

An article published in The Wave *of cember* 24, 1897.

Cosmopolitan San Francisco

White Land there must have been a tremendous crowding force along in the middle of the century, crowding the Russians up and up and up on to the shoulder of their country till they slid off and over into Alaska. They spread phenomenally and came steadily southward. There is even record of a clash between them and the early settlers. Sutter's fort, so an old guardian of the place once told me, was built ostensibly against the Indians, but in reality to resist the encroachment of the Russians. The Russian himself has left indications of himself in a blockhouse or two or a fort or two, and even in the geographical names such as the *Russian* River. But no doubt the Alaskan purchase checked immigration from that quarter.

The aggregation of "little" Mexico, Italy and the like that makes a place for itself in San Francisco lies over on the other side of Chinatown and beyond the Barbary Coast. A good way to reach it is to follow the alleys of Chinatown, beginning at Waverley Place and going on through Spofford Alley and Gamblers' Alley, till you come out near Luna's restaurant. Strike out in any direction from Luna's and in a sense you will travel a thousand miles at every step. The best time to see "The Quarter," as Anglo-Saxon San Francisco has come to call the place, is on a Saturday evening, between seven and eight o'clock, along in August or early September. "All the world" is on the streets at that time, and not a store has its shutters up. The very fruit stalls are open for business.

An article published in The Wave of December 24, 18

There is no suggestion of the Anglo-Saxon; neither in the speech of the sidewalk strollers, nor in the shop windows, nor in the wording of signs and advertisements; nor, fortunately in the general demeanor and behavior of the people. They are wine-drinkers essentially, and they know how to drink. There must be some—as yet unexplained—connection between malt drinks and truculence. Occasionally—at large intervals—an inhabitant of San Francisco's Quarter knifes or pistols his fellow, but there is no fighting in the Quarter. The Latin is disputatious rather than quarrelsome, and when angry with his brother, with or without cause, prefers unostentatious murder to brutal thumpings, swung chairs and hurled bottles.

Then, too, our Mexicans, Italians and other people of the Quarter, take their pleasure in a different way. It is a grim and significant fact that when the German and the Irishman set about their amusement they go away from their homes. The Irishman, besides, goes away from his wife and children—one is speaking now of the mass of them. He forgathers with individuals of his own sex and disports himself in saloons and bars and the public parks, and his enjoyment is not complete unless he embroils himself in a fight. The German organizes interminable, more or less solemn, "basket picnics" on Sundays, locks up

An article published in The Wave *of* December 24, 1897.

his house and goes "across the bay" for the day. You may see these families coming home by the score on any of the ferry boats late Sunday afternoon. The children's hats are stuck full of oak leaves, and the lunch baskets are crammed with wilted wildflowers.

The Latin inhabitant of San Francisco's Quarter takes his holiday at home. He—or she—lives in the street. Even when indoors the windows are wide open. The doorstep and open windows answer the purposes of the club. They are coigns of vantage where one may see the world go by. The women on the doorstep, the men on the sidewalk and the children in the street, is the arrangement most frequently met with.

On Sundays, the Anglo-Saxon goes to the country, the Latin goes to church and to mass. In the afternoon he amuses himself *chez lui*, goes to the theater, if he can, and crowds the gallery if there be an opera in town. In the evening he dines with his family at a restaurant, staying there, be it understood, until bedtime. Occasionally you will find him in one of the Bocce courts underneath Telegraph Hill, absorbed in the game, which one is inclined to believe is the stupidest game ever conceived by the mind of man.

Little Japan is more scattered, Yokohama is broken into bits of marquetry and set here and there in San Francisco, in back courts and *cul de sacs* and streets that have no outlet. The Jap is too eager for Western customs to keep his individuality long. He becomes Americanized as soon as he may. However, he organizes fencing clubs, which seem to be quite a feature of his social life among his fellows. On Sundays these clubs meet, (there is one of them in a court off Geary street, not far from Powell, and another in a small Japanese colony in Prospect Place, off Pine, between Powell and Stockton streets). The Japs get into their native regalia and fence with bamboo swords from dawn to dark. It is a strange idea of amusement, but no stranger than the Celt's love for actual fighting.

And the Chinaman. One leaves him to the last, for the sake of the last word, if ever there can be a last word said of the Chinaman. He is in the city but not of it. His very body must be carried back to Canton after his death, whither his money has gone already. He has brought to San Francisco and implanted here the atmosphere of the Mysterious East, that—short stories and Chinese plays to the contrary—must always remain an unknown, unknowable element to the West. No two races the world round could be more opposite than the Mongolian and Anglo-Saxon that are placed side by side in the streets of this strange city of the Occident. The Saxon is outspoken, the Mongolian indirect; the one is frank, the other secretive; the one is aggressive, the other stealthy; the one fears neither God, man nor the devil, the other is ridden with superstitions; the one is brusque, the other

An article published in The Wave *of* December 24. 189

*An article
published in
The Wave of
December 24, 1897.*

patient to infinity; the one is immoderate, the other self-restrained. But—it is well to remember this—the Chinaman is high-tempered and passionate to a degree, with finely-tempered nerves and much more sensitive temperament than the Westerner would care to give him credit for. His policy of self-repression is deceiving. In every Chinaman there is something of the snake and a good deal of the cat. If one knew him better one would hesitate longer before injuring him. He remembers things. The Presbyterian Mission is all very well, the police force and special detectives are all very well, but we can never know anything of the real Chinaman, can never have any real influence upon him, either to better his moral condition, or punish his crimes. Where else, in what other city in the world, could the Tongs fight with impunity from street to street? Where else would Little Pete have been shot to death in a public place and his murderers escape beyond all hope of capture?

With the Chinaman curiosity is considered a vice—almost a crime. Chinatown in San Francisco is as foreign to us—much more so—than a village in the interior of France or Spain. As a consequence Saxon visitors must be equally foreign in the eyes of the livers in Chinatown. If you went through a hamlet in France or Germany, far enough off the railroad, you would be stared out of countenance. Every doorway and window would be filled after your passage, and the very dogs would bark at your heels. But how is it with the visitor in Chinatown? Get down into the very lowest quarter, where the slave-girls are kept, where the Cantonese live, where Chinatown is most Chinese. Of the hundreds of silently shuffling China-men, not one will turn to look at you—they will hardly make way for you. You may go into their shops, their tea houses, their restaurants, their clubs, their temples—almost into their very living rooms— to those thousands of slit-like, slanting eyes you do not so much as exist.

An article published in The Wave *of* December 24, 1897

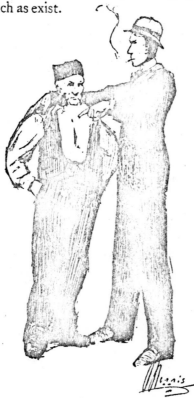

A drawing by Frank Norris from the University of California Blue and Gold, 1894.

Reviews & Interviews

ARTICLES REPRINTED FROM

The Wave of 1896 and 1897.

I. *Fiction in Review*

Published in The Wave of July 18, 1896.

Three new novels come to hand: "In a Dike Shanty," by Maria Louise Pool (Stone & Kimball), "His Honour and a Lady" (Appleton & Co.), by Sarah Jeanette Duncan, and "Chronicles of Martin Hewitt" (Appleton & Co.), by Arthur Morrison.

Mr. Morrison's collection surprises me. That the man who wrote "Tales of Mean Streets" could descend to such crude, unoriginal, really amateurish compositions as these "Chronicles" is not to be explained. Of course it is just possible that the tales may have been written prior to Mr. Doyle's "Sherlock Holmes" stories, and, for Mr. Morrison's sake, I hope they were. However, I am afraid it is quite the other way about. You lay down the "Chronicles" with a feeling of indignation. The idea of the series is palpably, openly cribbed from Doyle. They are detective stories, bad detective stories at that. Martin Hewitt is but a copy of Holmes and Brett a feeble reproduction of his friend who accompanies him on all his adventures and relates them afterward.

A Review published in The Wave *of* *July* 18, 1896.

There is nothing new or original in any of the tales. If you have not read of Sherlock Holmes' adventures you may be interested in Martin Hewitt; but if you are familiar with the doings of that famous amateur you will not find these chronicles worth their ink.

Mrs. Coates' "His Honour and a Lady" is something better. It is a tale of modern city life in India, most of the characters being the officers and employees of the civil service and their wives and daughters. It is a bit dreary, I find, in spite of all its intrigue. Mrs. Coates is too literary in fact. One feels that there has been a polishing and a repolishing of the whole matter, a refining and filing down as it were, to twelve places of decimals until the verve and spontaneity, the life of the thing, in a word, has been quite covered up and lost under an exquisite cold veneer. It is impossible not to compare this elaborate study of Indian society with the rapid *ebauches* of Mr. Kipling flung off at white heat, crammed with living, breathing things, with no execrable "literary finish" to hide the true, honest grain of human life underneath. Mrs. Coates' novel makes fair reading, however, if one can be satisfied with its literature, or can forget it.

"In a Dike Shanty," by Maria Louise Pool, is a novel—no, not a novel, nor yet a tale, nor collection of tales, but rather a picture of life, precisely the reverse of Mrs. Coates' production. "His Honour and

*A review
published in*
The Wave *of
July* 18, 1896

/

a Lady" is essentially a work of the closet. The author
sitting apart at her desk watching the world go by
through her windows. But it's a hundred dollars to a
paper dime that the author of a "Dike Shanty" actually lived the life she writes about. I honestly believe
she and Caroline Branson did buy a tract of Dike.
I believe in Orlando the terrier, in Mar Baker's
"idjit," and in Rodge Peake's wife's niece. I believe
in the tract of Dike and the flat grass land and the
wind and the shanty and the hayricks. It's fine, and
if there is little composition in it, little arrangement,
or the pulling of concealed strings, there is at least
the breath of real life. "In a Dike Shanty" is just
what it pretends to be—a picture of open-air life on
the New England coast, or rather a series of pictures,
one for each short chapter, loosely held together by
the little love affair of Leife and "Miss" Vance.

A romance may, of course, have excitement and
brilliancy and any number of attractive things, but
there is one quality it absolutely must have—that
which prevents you from putting it down when you
have once begun it. In this Elizabeth Knight Tompkins has succeeded very pleasantly in her new novel,
"The Broken Ring." (G. P. Putnam's.) The danger
is nowhere uncomfortably thrilling, nor the mystery
bewilderingly dark, but there is just enough of both
to keep one well absorbed until it all comes out right
in the last chapter. There are some very pretty love

scenes towards the end, notably the one in the park, where the broken ring and what the parrot said figure. The book is essentially a light one, more appropriate to a lazy afternoon than a serious morning, and must be taken as literary lemonade rather than beef tea or absinthe—pleasant and refreshing, with no lasting effects.

A review published in The Wave *of* *July* 18, 1896.

II. *Millard's Tales*

Mr. F. B. Millard of the San Francisco "Examiner" is out with a collection of stories—some fifteen of them—which the Eskdale Press publishes under the general title of "A Pretty Bandit." In telling his yarns Mr. Millard has adopted the method employed by the latest successful short-story men. This is not to tell a story, but to strike off an incident or two clean-cut, sharp, decisive, and brief, suggesting everything that is to follow and everything that precedes. The method is admirable, but it demands an originality and ingenuity on the part of the author that is little short of abnormal. The "motif" of the story must be very strong, very unusual, and tremendously suggestive. More than this, it must be told in sentences that are almost pictures in themselves. The whole tale must resemble, as one might say, the film of a kinetoscope, a single action made up from a multitude of viewpoints. In choosing this method Mr. Millard

A Review published in The Wave *of* *August* 21, 1897.

Millard's Tales

*A review
published in
The Wave of
August 21, 1897.*

has volunteered to enlist in the army of the strongest story-writers the world 'round, and some of his stories are quite good enough to bring him well up in the front ranks, notably the "Caliente Trail," "A Notch in a Principality" (to our thinking the best story of the book), "The Girl Reporter," and "Horse-In-The-Water." It is a dodge of publishers, as everyone knows, to put the two best stories at the beginning and end of such a collection. But there is little in "A Pretty Bandit" and "The Making of Her" to commend them. Mr. Millard crystallizes a most startling experience in each of these tales, but somehow fails to convince the reader of its "probability"; as, for instance, the hold-up in the first-named story. That a girl should stand up a stage is extraordinary enough for the most sensational-loving reader, but that she should do so upon the impulse of the moment is quite beyond belief—even worse, it is inartistic. In "The Making of Her" (which came very near being the marring of her) Mr. Millard has evidently striven for a contrast of types, the Boston bluestocking and the Western cowboy. The contrast is sharp enough, but the "events" narrated are not plausible. They all could have happened, it is true, but in story-telling the question is "might" they have happened? One can forgive the impossible, never the improbable. As a whole, however, the tales make capital good reading. Mr. Millard wastes no time—

his own nor his readers—in getting down at once to the heart of his work. There is a plainness, a directness in his style that is "the easy reading and hard writing" one has heard so much about. The author has confined himself to California material, which is always good policy, and at the same time impresses his readers with the fact that he is thoroughly posted upon whatever subject is under consideration for the moment, whether it be railroad life, newspaper life, camp life, or ranch life. ("A Pretty Bandit," F. B. Millard. The Eskdale Press, New York.)

A review published in The Wave *of August 21, 1897.*

III. *Lackaye "Making-Up"*

After I had waited a few minutes in the "star's dressing-room," Mr. Lackaye entered in a great hurry. Indeed, everything that went on during that half hour of preparation seemed to be done in a hurry. Wilton Lackaye hurried through the endless details of his wonderful make-up; members of the company hurried in to receive hurried directions, and hurried out again to follow them; a wig-maker hurriedly displayed a number of wigs and was hurried off without ceremony; a certain young man, whether he was a supe or a valet I could not make out, removed Mr. Lackaye's shoes in a great hurry, and hurried on Dr. Belgraff's carpet slippers, while at every moment a sceneshifter made a sudden appearance at

An interview published in The Wave *of December 5, 1896.*

Lackaye Making Up

*An interview
published in
The Wave of
December 5, 1896.*

the dressing-room door exclaiming in breathless excitement: "Five minutes more," and a little later:
"Orchestra on." Then at succeeding intervals:

"Overture."

"Curtain up."

"Mrs. Lackaye on."

All this while Wilton Lackaye, the pivot about whom everything revolved, was at one moment talking and laughing with Miss Fuller's manager, at another making suggestions to a younger actor as to his wig in "Moliere" (next week's play), or abusing a recalcitrant shoemaker over the fit of a certain pair of shoes, or again talking to me as to "make-ups," theories of acting and the difference between his methods and those of Coquelin and Irving. Not for an instant, however, did he pause in his work of transforming himself from the rotund, well favored American that he is into the blonde, whiskered German Herr Doktor—Roentgen it is, so Mr. Lackaye says.

"There are two theories of acting," said Wilton Lackaye, carefully modeling the pink, putty-like false nose before the glass, as cleverly as any sculptor. "There is the actor who says, 'It will be all right on the night,' and who relies upon the hysteria (note that Mr. Lackaye calls it hysteria; that's a curious word in such connection) the hysteria of the occasion to carry him through. They call it inspiration. Maybe it is inspiration. I've nothing against it. And—"

An interview published in The Wave *of* December 5, 1891

The nose was about finished, and Mr. Lackaye smeared his face plentifully with grease paint and rubbed some vermilion stuff—it was crude vermilion —around his eyes and cheeks. "And there is the other kind of actor" (the false nose made his tone a little nasal) "who relies almost entirely upon the careful manipulation of his mechanical effects to—Eh, what do you want? (the wig-maker had approached him). No; a servant would not wear puffs at the side of his wig like that; take it away and change it.— Relies almost entirely upon the careful manipulation of his mechanical effects—"

"I say, Governor" (this from a dignified old gentleman made up as a doctor, who put his head in the door) I say, can we have the California to-morrow for the rehearsal of "Captain Bob"?

"Curtain up," called the stage hand over the old gentleman's shoulder.

Mr. Lackaye had just finished gluing on the chin part of his beard; now he was putting on the remainder over his cheeks in little patches, "so as not to interfere with the play of the facial muscles," he explained to me in an aside. " 'Captain Bob' here," he said to the dignified gentleman, " 'Moliere' at the California. As I was saying," he continued, adjusting the auburn wig and blackening his eyelids, "relies altogether upon his mechanical effects. But they make the mistake—pass me that sponge—of suppos-

An interview published in The Wave *of December 5, 1896.*

ing that the one must exclude the other. Now I—" he pinned a lock of his real hair to that of the wig with a couple of invisible hairpins, and smeared the spot gray—"now I hold that the two methods should go together, first your detail, your mechanics and effects and make-up; then the fine frenzy is right enough when it comes."

The curtain had been up and the play progressing fully five minutes. Mr. Lackaye had only finished making-up his face and was still in his street dress. I thought of amateur performers ready an hour before and waiting for their cue in an agony of excitement. From time to time the star's dresser stepped to the door, cocking an ear in the direction of the stage. He drew out Lackaye's costume—Dr. Belgraff's woolen shirt, stained trousers and apron. It did not seem possible that the actor could get into them and out upon the stage in time. I began to get horribly nervous, began to wish he would stop wasting breath talking to me and attend to business. The dresser hurried him into his clothes. Mrs. Lackaye had long since disappeared; we could hear her voice from the direction of the stage. While the big white apron was being fastened, Lackaye was chaffing with Miss Fuller's manager. By this time I was absolutely certain that his cue was long past and Miss Wainwright was holding the stage for him. In another minute I should have had nervous prostration.

"Denver really surprised us," said Lackaye. "We did not count on large fronts there, but—"

"All ready, Mr. Lackaye," cried the call boy from the door. In an instant Wilton Lackaye—I mean Dr. Belgraff, for the transformation was absolutely beyond belief—was gone, the dresser running after him tying the last knot on the apron strings. He disappeared under the stage, and just in time, just by the fraction of a second came up through the cellar door and out on the stage in response to his cue, as calm and as absolutely master of himself as if he had been listening for it throughout the whole previous hour, rehearsing his opening speech the while.

An interview published in The Wave *of December* 5, 1896.

IV. *Mrs. Carter at Home*

One was rather awestruck with No. 50. It was the kind of hotel room at which one rings, not knocks, and thereafter is "ushered into an ante-chamber" by the maid. Inside, beyond the ante-room, where three Gargantuan trunks, bundles (not bunches, you know), bundles of flowers, and Mrs. Carter, Mrs. Carter who of late has become so celebrated on account of her fame.

An interview published in The Wave *of August* 14, 1897.

Laura Jean Libby would have said that Mrs. Carter was dressed in "some soft, clinging stuff"; and so, precisely, she was; lace like soapsuds and silk that had a glimmer on it like wet asphalt. But that dress, or

An interview published in The Wave *of* August 14, 1897.

Mrs. Carter at Home

tea-gown, or peignoir (of course it wasn't a peignoir, though), or whatever it was, had as much form and shape as a spilled plate of mush. It was all blooming mass and color, no outline at all, and on top of this heap of pale, indeterminate tints Mrs. Carter's hair flamed up with an effect that was somehow brusque and abrupt, as if some one had suddenly turned up the gas.

Mrs. Carter is very tall; carries that gold-girdled head of hers six feet from the ground, I'm thinking, and is very graceful in a strange, stiff way—just as a tall, stiff reed is graceful. But she is not pretty to my notion. No, as I recall her, she is not pretty. One would have had her face a little fuller and not quite so tired looking, and her nose might have been a little littler, and her eyebrows not so heavy. But I suspect one sees Mrs. Leslie Carter at a disadvantage when she is off the stage. She impressed me as if seen out of her element in No. 50. I was continually drawing an imaginary line of footlights between us. We sat down, Mrs. Carter with her back to the mirror. Interviewing Mrs. Carter is interviewing made easy, for she did all the talking. There was nothing for me to do but to put in an occasional word, just to keep her going. I suppose she has been interviewed so much, poor lady, that she knows just what to say without being asked. Some wretch, I think, must have told her to be ready on the subject of "climate," for she started

An interview published in The Wave of, *August* 14, 1897.

off on that with a rush, and had got so far as fruits and flowers before I could stop her. All through our talk she was continually bolting up that worn, worn road.

Never have I seen an actress so anxious over her reception. Mrs. Carter asked me all manner of questions as to the temper of San Francisco audiences, regularly interviewed me on the subject, and seemed mighty ill at ease over the matter of the four weeks' run of the "Heart of Maryland."

"I am absurdly superstitious," says she. "You know I'm from the South, from Kentucky, and I believe in omens and signs and all the rest, but only in the bad ones, in the ill-omens. I suppose it's safest. Do you know," she exclaimed, suddenly, "I believe your fogs out here are actually doing my voice a world of good. Oh, this cli—"

I leaped into the breach. "Your voice!" I shouted. "Fogs, you say! Now that's curious."

"Why, I've been working ever since 10 this morning (at this time it was after 7) with my voice raised all the time, and I'm not a bit hoarse. Do you think I'm hoarse?"

I spread my palms toward her.

"No, not in the least," she went on. "Now, nowhere else could I do that. And Monterey? Oh, talk to me about Monterey and Del Monte! I went there for a rest, you know, and the weather there (the danger

An interview published in The Wave *of* *August* 14, 1897.

Mrs. Carter at Home

flag was out) was absolutely perfect. Oh, I shall live in California some day. Such a climate I never—(I knew it was coming.)

"Yes, of course," I shrieked. "Talk to me about the 'Heart of Maryland.' Don't you swing from the clapper of a bell somewhere?"

Mrs. Carter put this aside lightly.

"Yes, yes, but that's just a little sensation. I like this play, this Maryland, better than any play I ever acted in" (caution—they all say this of their latest play, so make allowances), "and you know I don't say it for mere advertising effect" (they always add this remark, too), "but the more I play it the better I like it. The climax of the second act is really one of the strongest things on the American stage. I do so hope you will like the play."

"Of course I'll like it," said I.

"If a hammer falls behind a flat during a scene you won't," said Mrs. Carter, "and if a calcium light doesn't go just right you'll say the piece lacks 'unity of conception.' Oh, I know what critics are. And on first nights with the best management some one little thing is sure to happen. I wish we could do away with first nights and begin with seconds, or even thirds."

"Or with the last night and work backward."

And with this I got up and worked backward myself toward the door.

"If you like 'Maryland' come and see me again and tell me about it," said Mrs. Carter.

"And if I don't like it?"

"Then you mustn't come."

"I shall be frantic in my enthusiasm Monday night," said I.

V. *Belasco on Plays*

An interview published in The Wave of August 28, 1897.

I don't need to go to see the "Heart of Maryland" now. I say that I don't need to go, but I want to more than ever. Maybe you don't quite understand the apparent contradiction here, but you would if you had been with me the other day in a little room over the ticket office of the Baldwin and heard Mr. Belasco himself tell the story of the play, of how he came to write it and how he actually did write. Incidentally, Mr. Belasco told me of his methods in general and his views on the drama.

It was most interesting to hear him tell the story of the fourth act of "Maryland." It was at once a pantomime—for he acted each part; a story—for he filled in the pauses of the dialogue with description and scene-plot, for he made one see the different shifts and changes, and the location of every flat and property. It was better than being behind the scenes. It was behind even behind-the-scenes. It was right in the midst of things—in the author's brain. I confess I had come prejudiced against the curfew-shall-not-ring-to-night affair even before seeing the play; but

An interview published in The Wave *of August 28, 1897.*

as Mr. Belasco told of the careful and painstaking preparation for that very effect, it seemed to me the most natural thing for the lady to do under the circumstances. You say the thing was suggested to Mr. Belasco by the poem; very well, the lady in the play may have had the poem in mind herself. How do you know?

"It's the careful preparation that makes all the difference between melodrama and drama," said Mr. Belasco.

"As how?" said I.

"Preparation for your effects; gradual, natural, leading up to them, coaxing your audience step by step till you have them just where you want, and then spring your effect, and not until then. I always take my audiences into my confidence, as it were, this way. The actors in the drama need not know what's to happen, but the audience know. I tell them in one way or another. For instance, when my hero is a prisoner in the bell tower not a single man, woman or child from pit to dome but knows that he is to escape, that the play is to end with the union of the lovers. It's just a question of means. So I introduce the Provost Marshal complaining of the inefficiency of firing guns as a signal for escaping prisoners, and his suggestion as to the ringing of the bell. Then, too, I show them what happens when a prisoner tries to escape and fails. All the preceding act, too, is "treatment"

An interview published in The Wave of August 28, 1897.

for that bell scene. It's the only way to make a scene effective.

"As to your idea of play-making, now," I suggested.

"I write a play around either some central scene or some central idea. 'Maryland' I wrote around the climax of the second act. The 'Wife' around the scene where the husband of the unfaithful Helen Truman tells her to turn to him in her trouble. The 'Charity Ball' was written around an idea. The idea that a girl once unvirtuous is not necessarily bad thereafter; can, in fact, become the honest wife of an honest man."

I asked Mr. Belasco about the problem plays. He shook his head. "Failures every one, the public won't have 'em. They won't be touched in the raw. They come to the theater to see an amusing play, not a moral dissection with lancet and scalpel. There's Ibsen, of course, but Ibsen is a dramatist whom people read. Staged, his plays would fail surely and inevitably." Also, Mr. Belasco told me something surprising. "The problem play," said he, "is easy writing, easiest kind of play-writing. There are no effects, no great scenes; it's all discussion, discussion, discussion; the author leads up to nothing, has no great climaxes; he can, as you might say, write till he gets tired—or the audience does—and then ring down. No," said Mr. Belasco, "give me the play of great, strong, universal passions, love and hatred, and re-

A California Artist

An interview
published in
The Wave of
August 28, 1897.

venge and remorse, and let the noble passions survive and triumph; get at the heart of mankind, under its vest, as you might say, and find out the beautiful, true nobility that's there. That's my religion, and because I do that is why I am sure that my plays are successful. And another point, these great human passions, there are a limited number of them after all. After the first score of great plays of the world had been written the dramatists began to be obliged to repeat themselves a little, to "lift," as it were, from their predecessors. Take it in real life, the identical same crises and scenes and situations are constantly reoccurring. There is no such thing as absolute originality nowadays. You are not original even in real life. Believe me, there is no situation however striking, whether on the stage of a theater or the stage of human existence, but what the changes have been rung upon it to infinity."

"Rung with a curfew bell?" said I. (Of course I didn't say it.) But the idea occurred to me. And, after all, Mr. Belasco is not far from right.

VI. *A California Artist*

An Interview
published in
The Wave of
February 6, 1897.

Peters met us at the gate, standing on the steps that were the vertebrae of a whale. He was booted to the knee, and wore a sweater and a sombrero, and looked just as picturesque as I had hoped and ex-

*An interview
published in
The Wave of
February 6, 1897*

pected an artist should look. I suppose one is always on the lookout for pictures and scenes about an artist's habitat, and would persist in seeing them whether they existed or not. But at any rate I was rather impressed with all this, because it was unique and characteristic of a California artist. In Brittany he would have worn sabots and a beret, and perhaps a "blouse." In England it would have been a velvet jacket, but in Monterey, mark you, the artist wears a sombrero and high boots, and stands on steps that are the joints of a whale's spine. Where else would you see an artist with such attributes? We went into the studio.

Redwood, unfinished, and a huge north light, a couch or two, a black dog, lots of sunshine, and an odor of good tobacco. On every one of the four walls, pictures, pictures, and pictures. Mostly moonlights, painted very broad and flat, as though with Brobding-nag brushes. And in one corner a huge panel-like painting very striking, a sheer cliff, tremendously high, overlooking a moonlit ocean. On the edge—but the very uttermost edge, you understand—a man standing, wearing a cocked hat and a great coat. There was nothing more, not a single detail, and the man was standing with his back turned, yet it was Bonaparte and St. Helena, beyond all shadow of doubt. Clever, you say? Enormously so, I say. A single huge broad "note," as it were, simple, strong,

An interview published in The Wave of February 6, 1897.

conveying but a single impression, direct as a blow.

Peters told me he was "going in" for moonlights. That's a good hearing for his style, as the art critic would say; is "admirably adapted" for those effects where all detail is lost in enormous flat masses of shadow. Just the effect to be seen on a moonlight night.

"You would be surprised," says Peters, "to see how many different kinds of moons there are." He illustrated what he said by indicating one and another of the sketches. "There is the red moon, when she's very low, and the yellow moon of the afternoon, and the pure white moon of midnight, and the blurred, pink moon of a misty evening, and the vary-tinted moon of the drawing. She's never the same. Here are two *ebauches*, made on succeeding days, at the same time, and from the same place. Yet observe the difference." There was, indeed, a tremendous difference. I became interested. "It's the specialists," Peters continued, "that 'arrive' now-a-days, whether they specialize on diseases of the ear, or on the intricacies of the law of patents, or on Persian coins of the 14th century."

"Or on pictures of moonlight," said I.

"Precisely; that's my specialty."

Peters lives in Monterey on a hill-top, and paints from dawn to dark. After dark he goes out and looks at the moon, and the land and the shore in her light, and at the great cypresses. He doesn't paint there. Just

An interview published in The Wave of February 6, 1897.

looks and looks, and takes mental photographs, as it were—impressions he remembers and paints the next day. Singularly enough Peters, though going in for moonlights, does not paint them *en plein air*—how could he, for the matter of that, without any light to see by—but he does take a sort of combination note and sketch book along with him. He showed this to me. Here and there were mazes of pencil scratching, and the pages are almost unintelligible to any one but Peters himself, and written over them and in them were such words as "blue," "carmine and cobalt," "warm gray," "sienna," "bitumen" and "red," etc.— notes merely to help along in the more finished picture.

Peters thinks Monterey should be a great place for artists. He has sketched nearly everywhere, and maintains that there is more artistic "stuff" right down there in the old town than there is in Barbizon, even, or in the artist towns of Brittany. A few artists, in fact, have already "discovered" the place—artists that who since have been "Medailles" and have acquired greatness. Harrison himself, that Alexander the Great of marine painters, was here for a time, and Julian Rix, and Tavermeir and others, but none of whom have studied, really studied—in a careful, almost scientific fashion—the moonlight effects of the place as has Peters. There are two ways of painting a moonlight sky—one as I have seen it done by scores

*An interview
published in
The Wave of
January 6. 1897.*

of artists hitherto, who paint in the sky a sort of indeterminate dark gray or very "warm" black. The
other way is as Peters does it. Night skies are blue—
deep, deep blue. Look into the sky the next time you
are out at night. Maybe you thought the sky was
black at night. Look at it. Blue! of course it's blue—
bluer than the bluest thing you ever saw. But I never
noticed the fact until Peters' pictures called my attention to it.

The interior of Peters' house, by the way—not his
studio, but his house—is a picture in itself. He has a
wonderful collection of arms, furniture, carpets, china,
stuffs and the like—something really extraordinary.
There are old Delft mugs, and a chair of brocade silk
that Josephine once used at Malmaison, and a ship-
model of ivory presented to Bonaparte by the city of
Toulon, original editions of Buffon, worth more than
their weight in silver, and an old bed—one of the
boxed-in kind, with sliding doors—from Brittany,
that the guest still sleeps in—a marvel of carving,
with the genuine Breton bird and worm design upon
it, that stamps it at once as the rarest of curios.

I was wondering how large must have been the sum
that Peters was obliged to pay for the wonder, when
by one of those extraordinary coincidences that are
all the time happening, he said: "I gave the fellow
twenty-five dollars for that bed."

In the Heat of Battle

A DIALOGUE FROM

The Wave of December 19, 1896.

CHARACTERS: Jerry Tremont, *Yale '92.* Tressie Tremont, *his sister, a "Yale Girl." Lord Orme, (oxon.), a young English nobleman. "Jack," halfback on the Yale eleven, who does not appear but who is the most important of all.*

SCENE: *Office of Mr. Tremont, Sr., Newspaper Row, Boston, overlooking the street which is packed with an immense crowd. Directly opposite is the "Herald" building. Upon the front of the "Herald" building is affixed a huge bulletin board, on which appear half-minute bulletins of the Harvard-Yale football game, the second half of which is at that moment being played at Springfield, Mass. Lord Orme and Miss Tremont are sitting at the window to the right. Jerry is standing at the window to the left, which is open.*

Jerry (drawing back from the window and facing into the room)—No scoring in the first half, and the ball in the center of the field at the call of time. That's close work.

Miss Tremont (to Lord Orme after glancing down into the street)—Dear me, did one ever see such a crowd!

Lord Orme—It's jolly like Trafalgar Square on Lord Mayor's day.

Miss Tremont—I'm so sorry we couldn't see the game this year, but I suppose watching the returns is the next best thing.

In the Heat of Battle

*A dialogue
published in
The Wave of
December 19, 1896.*

Lord Orme—It was—ah—your uncle's death that prevented?

Miss Tremont—Um-hum; papa thought we hadn't better go. It was all we could do to get him to give us his office for to-day.

Jerry (calling from the other window)—Here's another bulletin.

Miss Tremont—Oh, read it for me, Jerry, will you? I can't (putting up her lorgnette) see even across the street. Isn't it a pity to have such eyes as mine, Lord Orme?

Lord Orme—I don't know about that, Miss Tressie. They've had a jolly queer effect on me—I—ah—

Jerry (reading the bulletin)—"Springfield, 3:28 P.M. Time called for second half. Harvard has the ball. Jack Harper will still play left half for Yale in spite—"

Miss Tremont (with sudden interest)—What's that about Jack?

Jerry—Jack's going to go on with the game just the same in spite of his shoulder.

Miss Tremont—Hurrah for Jack! (She catches Lord Orme's enquiring glance.) Jack—Mr. Harper—Well, Jack's a man I know. He plays for Yale.

Lord Orme (noting her confusion)—Is he "the other man," Miss Tressie?

Miss Tremont—"The other man?"

Lord Orme—There always is "the other man," you

A dialogue published in The Wave of December 19, 189?

know, Miss Tressie, in affairs—in—ah—affairs such as—such as ours. I mean, such as this.

Miss Tremont—Oh, why should you assume that he is "the other man," maybe—

Lord Orme—There must be "another man" somewhere. If it's not this famous Jack it must be——

Miss Tremont (daringly)—It might be Lord Orme.

Lord Orme (in delighted embarrassment)—Oh, I say, now, Miss Tressie.

Miss Tremont (quickly)—And then again it might not. So there you are, you see.

Lord Orme (after a pause, suddenly perplexed)—Are you—ah—making game of me, Miss Tressie? It's a bit rough, you know, because I care so very much—

Jerry (reading from the bulletins) — "Harvard punts for forty yards—Yale's ball on her thirty-five yard line—Jack Harper of Yale makes five yards around Harvard's end."

Miss Tremont—Bravo, Jack! (Apologetically to Lord Orme), Mr. Harper would have been so disappointed if he had not been able to play. He's a senior. This is his last chance.

Lord Orme—It's my last chance, Miss Tressie. If I sail on Monday I won't see you again before I go. I—ah—couldn't have chosen a worse time to say—to say things, than now, I suppose, but last night, with so many people around you, I couldn't get a chance, you know.

In the Heat of Battle

A dialogue published in The Wave *of December* 19, 1896.

(They talk in low tones, and cannot be overheard, except in fragments, by the absorbed Jerry. At first Miss Tremont's attention is equally divided between Lord Orme's speeches and the Springfield bulletins as read by Jerry; but little by little her interest wavers. Sometimes inclining toward the game as Yale is winning, sometimes toward Lord Orme as Yale seems to be giving ground.)

Jerry (reading)—"Brunt of Harvard makes three yards through Yale's center."

Miss Tremont (commenting)—Jack said Yale was weak in the center this year. (After a pause), I wish I knew just how to answer you, Lord Orme.

Jerry (reading)—"Jack Harper misses a clean tackle and allows Harvard to advance the ball seven yards."

Miss Tremont—I confess I like you immensely, Lord Orme. I don't see why I cannot tell you that frankly.

Jerry (reading)—"Yale recovers the ball and makes ten yards around Harvard's right end."

Miss Tremont—But I don't think I care enough for you to marry you.

Jerry (reading)—Yale makes three more yards through Harvard's tackle."

Miss Tremont—I'm sure I don't.

Jerry (reading)—"Yale gains another five yards."

Miss Tremont—Oh, quite sure.

*A dialogue
published in
The Wave of
December* 19, 18

Jerry (reading)—"Harvard gets ball on fumble and makes a long gain through Yale's center."

Miss Tremont—On the other hand, something might happen to make me change my mind. I—I—don't know just what to tell you.

Lord Orme—Devotion such as mine should go for something, Miss Tressie. I know it's an old argument, but I am sure you would care more for me in time.

Jerry (reading)—"Yale loses five yards for off-side play. Harvard still gaining through center."

Miss Tremont—(How I hate those Harvard men.) Y-yes, perhaps—I—I might, you know.

Jerry (reading)—"Jack Harper of Yale breaks through Harvard line and tackles runner for a loss—tremendous cheering on Yale bleachers." Good boy, Jack. That's the stuff.

Miss Tremont (laughing with sudden perverseness) —And then again I might not, you know.

Lord Orme (deliberately)—Miss Tressie, you and I have known each other a good bit now. You know, I'm sure, what you can expect of me. I'm not an intellectual, nor a physical giant, I confess, and I'm not what you Americans call smart, but our name is in Gotha and in Burke and all that sort of thing, and I can shoot straight and—and—and I can stick on anything that wears four hoofs—

Jerry (still reading)—"3:35 P.M.—Yale is losing ground. Harvard has the ball on Yale's twenty-five

In the Heat of Battle

A dialogue published in The Wave *of December* 19, 1896.

yard line. Yale does not seem able to stop Harvard's masses on tackles and guards."

Miss Tremont—I'm sure you undervalue yourself, Lord Orme. I hate smart people, and it don't follow that a girl must like a man just because he's big and strong, and I adore riding.

Lord Orme—As for that, Miss Tressie, there are about twenty thoroughbred hunters in my stables down in Surrey that are only waiting for you to ride them. Did you never ride to hounds? There's a proper jolly sport. I've a pack down there, too. It's not exactly the Quorn nor the Westminster, but it's a tidy little hunt of thirty couples, and they make music, I promise you, when they're in cry, and there's no end of foxes. We hunt twice a week in season.

Jerry continues reading in an agony of apprehension—"Yale is being driven back yard by yard. Harvard is still hammering the tackles with deadly effect. The ball is on Yale's fifteen yard line. Harvard bleachers wild with excitement."

Miss Tremont—Just think, if Yale should lose! No, I've never even seen a fox hunt, but it must be great fun.

Lord Orme—Talk about football!

Miss Tremont—I'm afraid it would almost be better than football, Lord Orme.

Lord Orme—I showed you the photograph of our town house, didn't I? It's close by the Row in Till-bury Circus. It's by Vanburgh. Fairfax owned it once. And, of course, we would arrange with the dowager—that's my aunt, you know—to have you presented.

Miss Tremont (then breathlessly)—And I should be presented—presented at court? Oh! This winter? At the next Drawing-Room?

Jerry (reading)—"The ball is now on Yale's five yard line."

Lord Orme—Of course, Miss Tressie, though perhaps not at the very next Drawing-Room. I should wish to have the estate well settled up before we returned to London society.

Miss Tremont—Settled up?

Lord Orme—Things are tangled a bit. Of course—ah—(hesitating and blundering) there are—there are—ah—a few debts.

Miss Tremont (her suspicions suddenly aroused by his embarrassment)—Debts! Is that why you have been talking like that to me, Lord Orme?

Jerry—"Harvard's advance suddenly checked. Yale rallies on her five-yard line."

Lord Orme (hastily)—Don't misunderstand, Miss Tressie. Believe me, I do care for you, for yourself as much as for your money—more, I mean. But even looking at it in the worst light, after all, is it taking any unfair advantage of you? Consider the return. You would have a position and a name in London society second to but very few. Think of the town

A dialogue published in The Wave *of* December 19, 189

A dialogue published in The Wave *of December* 19, 1896.

In the Heat of Battle

house, and the country seat in Surrey—and all the hunters and the fox hounds—and then you' know there's the yacht at Cowes—and you'd be presented —and—and hang it all, Miss Tressie, I really do care awfully, y'know. I say, now, Miss Tressie, we haven't got time to put this thing off—we've got to settle it this afternoon. I'll leave you to think it over for half an hour. I'll take a stroll in the Mall or the Common or whatever it is, if I can get through this bally crowd, and come back in half an hour for your answer. What do you say, Miss Tressie?

Miss Tremont (reflectively)—Well, all right, I'll think it over.

Lord Orme—Right you are. In half an hour I can have your answer?

Miss Tremont—Yes—I think so. (Exit Lord Orme).

Jerry (hearing the door close, turns from the window)—Hello, where's Orme gone? What's the matter, Tress? You look flustered.

Miss Tremont (aroused from a reverie into which she has fallen)—Hum? What, what is it, Jerry? Flustered? Well, I should say so. Aren't you?

Jerry (groaning)—I can't bear to watch the bulletins any more. Harvard's going to win. We can't keep 'em from it. Yale's asleep. Jack hasn't done a thing yet.

Miss Tremont—Oh, Jack's not in it any more.

Jerry—Eh! What—you say that of Jack? You?

*A dialogue
published in
The Wave of
December 19, 1891*

Say, Tressie, that's Orme's "fine Italian hand," I can see that.

Miss Tremont—Never you mind, Jerry.

Jerry—Look here, Tress, I know how Jack feels about you, and I don't propose you shall turn him down for any title, if I can help it. What's Orme been saying to you?

Miss Tremont—Oh, things and—and—things.

Jerry—For instance.

Miss Tremont—He's coming back for his answer in half an hour.

Jerry—You let it go as far as that?

Miss Tremont (her chin in the air)—Well?

Jerry—And what do you propose telling him?

Miss Tremont—I haven't made up my mind yet.

Jerry—Of course you have, you know you're not going to marry Lord Orme.

Miss Tremont—Pooh! I haven't said so yet.

Jerry—Say so now, then.

Miss Tremont—Oh, don't bother me. What's that last bulletin.

Jerry—Hello, hello. Oh, I say, Tress, look at what's been going on while we've been talking. (Reads)— "Yale gets the ball on downs and punts out of danger." That's something like. Oh, Yale hasn't lost yet. Tressie, don't you do anything foolish now, and make a decision all in a moment that you'll regret your whole life. Look at the men themselves. Don't you

*A dialogue
published in
The Wave of
...cember 19, 1896.*

suppose that Jack's the best of the two? Why, he's big enough to make three or four Lord Ormes, and you know how much he cares for you, and I know how much you care for him and—hold on, here's another bulletin. (Excitedly). Look there, Tressie. (Reads)—"Yale's ball in center of the field. Jack Harper makes a twenty yard run around Harvard's left end." Listen to the crowd in the street shouting. That's the longest run of the day.

Miss Tremont—Well, of course, I care for Jack. It's not that I like Jack any less.

Jerry—Honestly now, isn't he the best old chap you—wait a minute, here's another—"Yale men playing like fiends; have just worked a trick on Harvard that has netted a gain of ten yards."

Miss Tremont—Splendid. Of course Jack's a dear. I never said he wasn't.

Jerry—Then why do you let Orme talk you out of it? Orme's just after your—

Miss Tremont—What's that next bulletin?

Jerry (in great excitement)—It's Jack again. Oh, Tressie, we'll beat 'em yet.

Miss Tremont—What, what did he do?

Jerry (reading)—"Yale has the ball on Harvard's twenty-five yard line. Jack Harper makes ten more yards around the end." And you said Jack wasn't in it.

Miss Tremont—I never said it.

Jerry—You did.

A dialogue published in The Wave *of* December 19, 1897

Miss Tremont—I never. Jack's all right.

Jerry—You bet—every time. Lord Orme, pooh! and his old hounds and his dowager and his debts.—Look there, look: "Yale is outplaying Harvard at every point."

Miss Tremont—He has got debts.

Jerry—And the governor's good money is to pay them off while—hold on: "Yale is on Harvard's twelve yard line."

Miss Tremont—Glorious—and his nose is too long.

Jerry—Oh, confound him and his nose, watch the game; here, look (more and more excited)—"Yale is on the ten yard line. Now on the eight. The Yale bleachers are yelling like mad"—I should think they would.

Miss Tremont (clasping her hands in excitement) —Oh, we must win now.

Jerry (shouting)—"Five yards."

Miss Tremont—Oh, Jerry, isn't it exciting. Oh, if I could only see it all. Oh, Jerry, if we should fumble now.

Jerry—Fumble nothing. Jack's there, and don't you forget it. Dear old Jack.

Miss Tremont—Dear old Jack.

Jerry—Hear the crowd in the street giving the Yale yell. Think of it at Springfield now. Can't you just, just hear 'em. Can't you hear the bleachers roaring—just like thunder, Tressie. That's better than a lot of mangy foxhounds yelping, ain't it?

*A dialogue
published in
The Wave of
December 19, 1896.*

Miss Tremont—You bet it is—Yale! Yale!

Jerry—Here's another bulletin. Yale's on the twelve-yard line. "Harper makes three yards through tackle." Only nine yards more. "Harper makes another gain." Yale's on the eight yard line; on the six; on the five; on the three, and—now—now—now—now—(at the top of his voice, and throwing his hat in the air)—Tressie, Jack's made the TOUCHDOWN! We've won! Oh, ain't it grand—ain't it glorious! Three times three for Yale! Say, Tressie, what's the matter with Jack Harper?

Miss Tremont—He's all right, you bet, every time.

(Enter Lord Orme, who stands mystified in the doorway).

Jerry—Who's all right?

Miss Tremont—Jack.

Jerry—Who?

Both together—Jack.

Lord Orme (with a puzzled smile)—Is this some sacred and religious rite, some mysterious incantation, that I've interrupted? Miss Tressie, your hair's tumbling down; your gloves are split; your hat is all awry; your cheeks red. If I may be permitted to use the word, you do look regularly—ah—regularly bloused. And to think this is the little girl who's to be presented at the next Drawing-Room.

Miss Tremont (shouting)—No it's not. Bother your old Drawing-Room. Can't you see? Jack's won the game.

The Puppets and the Puppy *A* DIALOGUE
from The Wave *of May* 22, 1897.

"There are more things in your philosophy than are dreamed of in Heaven and Earth."

CHARACTERS: A Lead Soldier. A Doll. A Mechanical Rabbit. A Queen's Bishop, *from the chessboard.* Japhet, *a wooden mannikin from Noah's Ark.* Sobby, *the Fox-terrier Puppy.*

SCENE: *A corner of the play-room carpet.*

TIME: *The night after Christmas.*

The Lead Soldier—Well, here we are, put into this Room, for something, we don't know what; for a certain time, we don't know how long; by somebody, we don't know who. It's awful!

The Doll—And yet we know—I think I can speak for all of us—we know that there is a Boy.

The Mechanical Rabbit (reflectively)—The Boy—the Boy—it's a glimpse into the infinite.

The Queen's Bishop—Boy, forsooth! There is no Boy, except that which exists in your own imaginations. You have created a figment—a vast, terrible, empty nothing, to complement your own imperfections. I have given great thought to the matter. There

A dialogue published in The Wave *of* May 22, 1897.

is, perhaps, a certain Force that moves us from time to time—a certain vague power, not ourselves, that shifts us here and there. All of us chessmen believe in that. We are the oldest and highest cult of you all. But even this—what shall I call it?—this Force, is not omnipotent. It can move us only along certain lines. I still retain my individuality—still have my own will. My lines are not those of the knight, or the pawn, or the castle, and no power in the Room can make them so. I am a free agent—that's what is so terrible.

The Doll—Ah, you think you've solved it all—you, with your science and learning. There is a Boy, and I am made in his image.

The Lead Soldier—And I.

Japhet—And I.

The Mechanical Rabbit—Yes, yes, the Doll must be right. Who else could have implanted within me this strange power of playing upon these cymbals? Somebody must have wound me up. I say it was the Boy.

Japhet—But, come now; let us consider a moment. One thing we can all agree upon. Some day, sooner or later, we shall be Thrown-away. It is the inevitable end of all toys. We shall be Thrown-away and go to the Garret. Then what?

The Doll—Dreadful question.

Japhet—This is what I believe: Some day I shall be Thrown-away and go on that last voyage to the

A dialogue published in The Wave *of May 22, 1897.*

Garret, but not forever. I look forward to a time when I shall be made of rosewood instead of common pine, and shall have a white shellac finish instead of this base coating of non-poisonous paint, and I shall live forever in a Noah's Ark of silver.

The Lead Soldier—What childish fallacy! It is against all reason to regard our lot as such infantile trickery. I, too, some day shall be Thrown-away, but my conception of immortality is no such child's play as this. No; in course of time I shall be re-melted and cast again to form another lead soldier, who in his turn shall be re-melted and re-cast, and so on and on, forever and ever.

The Queen's Bishop—Dreams! dreams! dreams! What butterflies you chase! What phantoms you hug! After I have been Thrown-away, I shall gradu-ally rot and decay, and fall to dust, and be finally absorbed by the elements——

The Doll—And lose your identity? Never! Listen to me. I feel that in me there are three individualities, each of them me, and a fourth which is of Me, yet not in Me—the Not-me. There is the sawdust, the kid, and the china—a trinity. Then there is that mys-terious something which cries "Papa! Mama!" when the Boy presses on my chest. This is the Not-me. This is the part of me that shall last after I'm Thrown-away. That is my conception of immortality.

The Lead Soldier (soliloquizing)—And each time I

A dialogue published in The Wave of May 22, 1897.

am re-melted and re-cast I become a finer soldier—larger, firmer on my base, more life-like. Thus the race is improved. Immortality is but the betterment of the race.

The Mechanical Rabbit (decisively)—When I am Thrown-away that's the end of me—it's annihilation.

The Lead Soldier (after a pause)—Tell me this: Why was Falling-down brought into the Room? Here is another thing we are all at one upon—that it is wrong to Fall-down. It displeases the Boy.

The Queen's Bishop (sotto voice)—The Force that moves us, you mean.

The Mechanical Rabbit—That's all very well. I can see how it is wrong, horribly and fearfully wrong, for the Lead Soldier to Fall-down, when the Boy sets him in his ranks and he Falls-down, he drags with him the whole line of other soldiers. The wrongdoing does not stop with himself—it communicates itself to others. It is a taint that progresses to infinity. But why should it be wrong for me to Fall-down? I hurt no one but myself.

The Queen's Bishop—It is wrong for you as well as for the Lead Soldier and myself. You can know nothing of the vast, grand scheme of the Room. Suppose I should Fall-down whenever I chose, and knock over, say, the king, or the castles—what a calamity it would be! It would disarrange the vast, grand plan of events. No, no; in keeping upright we are only

*A dialogue
published in
The Wave of
May 22, 1897.*

helping on the magnificent, incomprehensible aim of the Room. The same moral law applies to us all. What's wrong for one is wrong for us all.

The Lead Soldier—But what shall we say in a case like this: The other day the Boy took hold of the drummer of my squad, and twisted and bent his standard so that he could no longer stand. He put him in the line, and naturally he Fell-down. Then the Boy threw him away. Was it the drummer's fault, I ask? Why should he be punished for falling down, when the Boy himself twisted his standard? And again, I have heard of lead soldiers who never could stand because of some fault in the casting. Were they to blame? They were doomed before they were cast, and were Thrown-away afterward.

Japhet—Dreadful problem! Any day the Boy may pull off my standard and Throw me away.

The Queen's Bishop—We cannot understand these things, but there must be reason in them. But if you come to that, why are we here anyhow? I owe my existence to the turning lathe. Did I ask to be turned?

The Mechanical Rabbit—Or I to be made?

Japhet—Or I to be whittled?

The Doll—Or I to be stuffed?

The Lead Soldier—Or I to be moulded? If I had been given choice in the matter I would have chosen to be the general of my box, who sits on a horse that is rearing up, and points with his sword. Accident

A dialogue published in The Wave *of May 22, 1897.*

The Puppets and the Puppy

alone put him there. His lead is no better than mine, and his uniform is only paint-deep. In the re-melting, perhaps, he may be cast as a private and I as the general.

(Sobby, the Fox-terrier puppy, pushes open the door of the room with his nose. His eye falls upon the mechanical rabbit. He rushes at it, shakes it between his teeth, and in a few minutes has worried it to an unrecognizable mass of skin and springs. Then he turns upon the doll, whom he likewise destroys. He chews the head from Japhet, and, with a movement of his paw, knocks the lead soldier down the register. Then he growls and scrabbles over the Queen's Bishop till it, as well, tumbles down the register. The Queen's Bishop disappears, muttering, vaguely, something about the "vast, resistless forces of nature.")

Through a Glass Darkly—A DIALOGUE

from **The Wave** *of June* 12, 1897.

CHARACTERS: Tom, Dick, *and* Harry, *and (later)* Jack *(who is engaged to* Dolly Street*)*.

SCENE: *The bay window of a certain down-town club of San Francisco. Some half dozen young men are present, smoking and chaffing and discussing "whiskey-and-sodas." Directly opposite, on the other side of the street, are the windows of a fashionable milliner's.*

Tom (looking out of the window)—I wonder now how many women stop and look in at that milliner's window as they go by.

Dick—One in three is a good average.

Harry—If there was a bargain-sale sign out, they wouldn't go by at all.

Tom—Look—here comes a girl.

Dick—She's a stunner, too! But she's in too much of a hurry. Bet she don't stop.

Harry—Bet she does

Dick—Take you—how much?

Tom—Hurry up—she's almost in front.

Harry—Betcha dollar.

Dick—A dollar it is.

(Interval of breathless suspense.)

A dialogue published in The Wave *of* June 12, 1897.

Tom—Now she's right there. She's going by—no, she ain't. Wait a minute, now.

Dick—She's slowing up.

Harry—She's got her eye on that green bonnet.

Tom—And it's marked down.

Harry—She can't possibly go by that.

Tom—She is, just the same.

Dick—No, she ain't.

Harry—There — there — there — she's stopped — she's going up to the window. I say, you owe me a dollar, old man.

Dick (gloomily):—There you are. Wimin folk air powerful onsartin.

Tom—Look here. I'll tell what we'll do. I'll pick out a girl as I see her coming down the street—understand?—and you fellows will bet on whether she stops and looks in at that window or not. Dick, he'll be the bear—that is to say, he'll bet she don't stop, and Harry will be the bull—he'll bet she does. I choose to be the croupier.

Dick—And how about if she goes in?

Tom—Then that pays double—just like a natural in *vingt et un*. All clear?

Dick and Harry—Sure—clear's glass. Go on now, pick out a girl. Won't this one do that's coming—the one with the net bag?

Tom—Not at all. There's an art in this thing that you fellows don't appreciate. That girl's from the

A dialogue published in The Wave *of* *June* 12, 189~.

country. Look at her feet. She won't even look in. She's spent too much money in town already, as you can see from the size of her net bag. She won't even allow herself to look in. I won't choose her, because the chances are too much against Harry.

Dick—How about that one just behind. She's a city girl, no mistake—the one in a tailor-made gown and the black sailor?

Tom—Yes, we gamble on this one. "Here she goes and there she goes, and whether she stops or not nobody knows."

Dick—A dollar, hey?

Harry—A dollar each time.

(They put up their money, and the girl passes by without stopping.)

Tom—Dick wins. (Dick takes the money.) Hurry up, you fellows—here comes another. This is a shop-girl, or perhaps she runs a soda-water fountain in a candy-store. And still the little ball goes 'round.

Dick—Not enough salary to think of bonnets. She'll never stop in a thousand years. There's my dollar.

Harry—It's the very reason why she will. She dreams of those bonnets every night. I'll see your dollar and I'll raise you a half.

Dick—And fifty cents harder.

Harry—And fifty cents harder than that.

(The girl goes straight into the store, indifferently, without even glancing at the window.)

*A dialogue
published in*
The Wave *of
June* 12, 1897.

Tom—Harry wins double.

Dick (with an aggrieved shout)—She was the sales-lady for that store. I appeal from the decision of the referee—dirty work! Yah—fake! fake! (groans).

Harry—All bets go with referee's decision. I'll trouble you for that money, old chap.

Tom—Hello, here comes Jack. Shall we let him in?

Dick—He's engaged to be married to Dolly Street. He won't take enough interest in other girls even to bet on their weakness for bonnets.

Harry—He's to be married next week. It's about time he devoted himself to a study of a woman's interest in bonnets. Oh, I say, Jack, come over here and "join our merry throng"!

Dick (scornfully)—Skin game! Turn out the gas! It's a notorious swindle! But tell him what the game is, Tom.

(Tom explains at length.)

Jack (with intense interest)—I see—I see! It's great! I tell you what—I'll bet on whether she goes in or not. I'll be a plunger. I can only lose a dollar if she stops, but I stand to win two if she goes in.

Harry—Here comes a stunning looking girl. See, the one with the heavy veil. I'll bet she's pretty, if one could see her face. Do we take this one, Tom?

Tom—Messieurs, *fait votre jeu.*

(They all make their bets. The girl pauses a moment in front of the window, looking at the bonnets

*A dialogue
published in
The Wave of
June 12, 1897.*

and hats, starts on again, hesitates, and turns back and enters the store.)

Tom—Jack wins double.

Jack—I say, this is better than poker.

Dick (giving him the money)—That was a swell-looking girl, though.

Harry—Wish we could have seen her face.

Tom—There she is—look—in the window of the store. The saleslady is showing her a hat. She's looking over here.

Harry—Who, the saleslady?

Dick—No, you jay; the girl—that swell girl.

Jack—That's so. She's looking right up here at the window.

Tom—Think she sees us?

Harry—Why, of course; that's what she's looking for. She's looking at me.

Jack—No, it's me she's looking at.

Harry—You're all wrong. She can't see you, Jack, sitting where you are.

Jack—'Course she can (greatly excited). I say, I say, I say—look there, fellows—I think—I think, that—yes, she is—she's really smiling at me. Shall I smile back at her?

Harry (indignantly)—Don't you dare—that smile's mine.

Jack—Betcha five dollars it's not.

Harry—Betcha ten it is.

A dialogue published in The Wave *of* June 12, 1897.

Jack—I'll take that.

Dick—How you going to prove it?

Tom—I tell you. First Harry will wave his hand at her and see if she waves back at him, or bows. And then Jack will try. And the one she answers wins the money. Catch on?

Jack—That's a go. There's my ten dollars.

Harry—And there's mine.

Tom—Now, then, Harry, wave your hand.

Dick—And be just as charming and gracious as you know how.

(Harry waves his hand at the girl, who puts her chin in the air and turns away her head.)

Harry—All is lost but honor.

Tom—Hold on—Jack hasn't won yet. She may turn him down, too. It's up to you now, Jack.

(Jack tries. The girl smiles very prettily, nods her head at him and waves her gloved hand.)

Jack—Horray! She's mine! Harry, perhaps you can play mumblety peg, but when it comes to girls, you're out of the running! Gimme that ten dollars. Whatle you fellows have to drink?

Dick—Hold up a minute. Watch the girl. She's going to try on a bonnet, and is taking off her veil. Now we'll see if she's pretty or not.

Jack—She's radiantly beautiful—I feel that she is.

Tom—There, her veil's off—she is pretty. Look at her, Jack.

A dialogue published in The Wave *f June* 12, 189?.

Jack (looks and then drops into a chair with a gasp)—It's Dolly!

Dick—Who?—what?—Miss Street?

Tom—It is, for a fact. I say, Jack—I—we—look here old man. We've—I've acted like a damned fool, and if it'll do any good I'll apologize—I can't begin to say how cut up I am. I guess (turning to Dick and Harry) I guess I can speak for all of us—we've been a lot of beastly little cads, and—and—well, I'm downright ashamed of myself. Will you shake hands on that?

Jack (extending his hand)—That's all right; of course you—we didn't know it was—who it was. I don't know why in the world I didn't recognize the dress, but that was a new waist I guess, and the veil was so thick. I guess I'll go down and see Dolly as she comes out. Some of you fellows sign the card for me, will you? (Exit.)

(Tom, Dick and Harry, left to themselves, look ruefully at one another for a moment.)

Tom—This is what our 'cross-the-water cousins would call an oncommon jolly rum go.

Harry—No wonder she waved her hand at Jack. But, Lord! what do you suppose she thinks of me?

Dick—But do you think now she knew who it was?

Harry—You mean that she didn't recognize Jack, after all?

Dick—It's pretty far from here across the street, and through two panes of glass.

Through a Glass Darkly

A dialogue published in The Wave of June 12, 1897.

Tom—Would Dolly Street flirt with a man she didn't know, and she engaged to Jack?

Dick—Pooh! Would Jack flirt with a girl he didn't know and he engaged to Dolly?

Dick—Betcha five dollars she didn't recognize Jack.

Harry—Betcha ten dollars she did.

Dick—Take you.

*   *   *   *   *   *   *   *

(Five minutes later. Dolly Street, coming out of the milliner's, meets Jack at the door.)

Jack (confusedly)—Say, hello, Dolly! Did you—those fellows—we didn't know——

Dolly (surprised at seeing him)—Why, dear old Jack, where did you come from? I haven't seen you in an age!

The Isabella Regina

A DIALOGUE FROM

The Wave of November 28, 1897.

CHARACTERS: Alfred. Angelina. A Conductor. A Train Boy.

SCENE: *The rear coach of a passenger train between any city and any fashionable suburb.*

Angelina—How far are we from the city, Alfred?

Alfred—I don't know. We must cross the bay first. We go as far as Rockport on the train, you know, and we take the ferry for the city there. We're not far from Rockport now (looking out the window), be there in about twenty minutes.

Train Boy (in a Gregorian chant)—Cigars-Cigar-ettes-chewing-gum-'n-tabacco.

Alfred—Here, boy. Give me an Isabella Regina — I say Angelina, you don't mind if I buy a cigar do you—Sidney Spence told me this boy sold a cigar I musn't fail to try. Of course I won't smoke now.

Angelina—Why of course I don't mind, Alfred. It was only cigarettes you promised me about.

Alfred—I won't buy one if you say not.

Angelina—But I *want* you should, I love to see you happy.

Alfred—My angel. (To the boy.) Two for a quarter?

*A dialogue
published in
The Wave of
November 28, 1897.*

Boy—Twenty-five cents straight. (Alfred gives him twenty-five cents, and puts the cigar in his upper vest pocket.)

Alfred (proudly)—Angelina, I haven't smoked a cigarette in a week, and you know I can get twenty-five cigarettes for what I pay for one cigar.

Angelina (with enthusiasm)—You are heroic; you are noble, Alfred.

Alfred (magnificently)—Pooh!

The Conductor—Tickets.

Angelina—Tickets, Alfred.

Alfred—You forget, we are traveling on a pass, Angelina.

Angelina—That's so, I had forgotten. Don't it make you feel grand to travel on a pass, Alfred, just as though you were a Personage?

Alfred: (with superb indifference)—Not a bit.

Angelina (gazing at him with admiration)—That's because you're so used to it.

Alfred (with nonchalance)—I suppose so, perhaps; I never think much about it.

The Conductor (near at hand)—Tickets. (Alfred hands him the pass with exquisite unconcern, yawning and looking out of the window.)

The Conductor—You must sign this pass, sir.

Alfred (biting his yawn in two and turning to the conductor in some confusion)—What, I—I thought I did pass the sign, I mean sign the——

A dialogue published in The Wave *of* November 28, 1890

The Conductor (coldly)—Well, you didn't. Sign in ink—don't use your pencil.

Alfred (helplessly)—But I haven't any ink. (The conductor silently hands him his fountain pen.)

Angelina—How can you sign, Alfred, when the car shakes so?

Alfred—I don't believe I can.

Angelina—It will be all jigglety, like that signature on the Declaration of Independence. Don't you remember, the one that's so shaky, I can't recall the name. Was it Hopkins or Hancock? it's dreadfully jigglety. There was a fac simile of the Declaration of Independence on the wall at the seminary, and Miss Mix used to tell us that Mr. Hopkins—or Mr. Hancock's hand shook so because he was afraid of the British. I *can't* remember whether it was Hopkins or Hancock. (To the conductor.) Do *you* remember?

The Conductor—What!

Alfred (handing him the pass)—There you are. (The conductor takes up the pass and is moving away.)

Alfred—Hey there, conductor. (The conductor pauses.) You didn't give us any ferry tickets. I thought you always gave passengers tickets for the ferry, when you took up their railroad tickets. You always have before.

The Conductor (loftily)—We only give ferry tickets to passengers travelling at regular transportation

A dialogue published in The Wave of *November* 28, 1897.

rates, we don't give 'em to holders of passes. (Moves on crying "Tickets!")

Alfred (excitedly)—But I say—here—hey there, conductor.

Angelina—What's the matter Alfred. (Alfred gasps, turns pale and rolls his eyes wildly.) Alfred, my own boy, what is it. You are ill. Oh, I said you shouldn't eat so much of that terrapin stew.

Alfred (fumbling rapidly in one pocket after another)—Nothing, nothing, I—I—I (miserably) I'm afraid I haven't any money.

Angelina (blankly)—Oh!

Alfred (distracted)—How are we going to get across the bay to the city? We'll be at Rockport in a few moments. I gave my last change to the train boy for that Isabella Regina. I thought our pass was good to the city. Angelina, we are lost. I haven't a cent.

Angelina—Nor I. And I *made* you get that cigar. It's I that have brought you to this. Oh! Alfred, it's all my fault.

Alfred (bravely)—No, *I* am the one to blame, I, only.

Angelina—No, no. It's only your heroism that says that. It was all on my account.

Alfred—I won't allow you to say that, Angelina.

Angelina—But you wouldn't have bought the cigar if I hadn't made you. I insisted. You see if you had

A dialogue published in The Wave *of* November 28, 18.

got cigarettes yesterday instead of your after-dinner cigar you would have got twenty-five cigarettes for what you paid for that one cigar and you might have had a few cigarettes left by now and wouldn't have had to buy that Isabella Regina cigar and-then-you-would-have-had-a-quarter-left-and-we-could-have-got-over-to-the-city — and, *oh!* I'm so unhappy. (Chokes back a sob.)

Alfred (wildly)—Angelina, you break my heart: stop, I'll throw myself from the train in another moment.

Angelina (clutching him hysterically)—Alfred, you shall not. Calm yourself. Oh, what's to become of us now. (Alfred starts suddenly as an idea occurs to him, his pallor increasing.)

Alfred (with terrible calmness)—And this next boat is the last to-day.

Angelina—What do you mean?

Alfred (still with horrible calmness)—If we don't get this next boat, there is none other we *can* get till to-morrow morning, and we'll be obliged to stay over in Rockport all night.

Angelina (repressing a shriek)—Alfred, don't *say* it. It *can't* be true. What's to become of *me*. Everybody *knows* we came away together to spend the day out of town, and, if we stay away all night—why—why—oh, what is going to become of us now. This is—this must be some horrible dream.

194

A dialogue
published in
The Wave of
November 28, 1897.

Alfred (in desperation)—And all for the want of a quarter. I shall go insane in another minute.

Angelina—Oh! I know I shall.

Alfred (looking about him)—We must get a quarter.

Angelina—There's that old gentleman across the aisle. Suppose you go to *him*. You could ask him to accommodate you with twenty-five cents, and you could give him your note.

Alfred (wildly)—Ha, ha, my note for sixty days. What's the interest on twenty-five cents for sixty days.

Angelina—Maybe you could *sell* him something. I know (clapping her hands), sell him the *cigar*. The *Isabella Regina*.

Alfred (with enthusiasm)—Saved me again, Angelina; you are my good angel. (Rising.) I'm going to try. Wish me God-speed, Angelina. (They clasp hands.)

Angelina—I *know* you will succeed.

Alfred—I go. (He approaches the old gentleman, and engages him in a few moments' interview, unheard by Angelina.)

Alfred (returning)—Crushed! He don't smoke.

Angelina—What did he say?

Alfred—Said he was the third vice-president of the Anti-Nicotine League.

Angelina—We're lost.

The Brakeman (opening the forward car door with

*A dialogue
published in*
The Wave *of*
November 28, 189

a yell): Next staishn's Bra-rah-rah! (Remainder unintelligible.)

Alfred—We are almost at Rockport; what *can* be
done.

Angelina—Can't we *hire* a boat and row across the
bay?

Alfred—And how would we pay the hire, I should
like to know?

Angelina—If I only had some jewels to give a boat-
man. Just like they do in novels! Don't you remember that poem:

> "A chieftain to the highlands bound
>   Cried boatman do not tarry,
> And I'll give thee a silver crown
>   To row us o'er the ferry."

We had it to scan at the seminary, and "tarry" and
"ferry" don't rhyme, nor "bound" and "crown."
I never thought of that before.

Alfred—But what's to be done. (The train whistles
for Rockport and begins to slow down; the passengers
collect shawl-straps and satchels; the conductor re-
appears.)

Angelina—Here's the conductor, Alfred. Let's appeal to the conductor. Tell him you haven't enough
money to get across the bay with, and ask him for
tickets and tell him you'll send him the money to-
morrow.

The Isabella Regina

*A dialogue
published in
The Wave of
November 28, 1897.*

Alfred—He never would relent. Didn't you notice what a frigid brutal manner he had. He's just in the railroad's employ, and paid to collect fares. It's nothing to him that we can't get across the bay. He is a minion; what the newspapers call "the tool of the corporation."

Angelina—*I'll* talk to him. I'll throw myself upon his—

Alfred (severely)—Angelina!

Angelina— —his mercy.

Alfred—No, I'll face him.

Angelina—Not alone, Alfred. I'll be at your side. (The train stops with a backward jerk and a prolonged hiss of relaxed air brakes. The other passengers leave the car. Angelina and Alfred approach the conductor.)

Alfred (in a low tone to Angelina)—I—think I'm a little afraid of him; he acted like such a bear about the pass.

Angelina—Be brave, Alfred.

Alfred (to the conductor, assuming a careless tone and speaking very loud)—I say, about those tickets across the ferry; I find myself in a very embarrassing situation (explains at length).

Angelina—And this is the last boat to-day, and—and—we're not—we're *going* to be married but—

The Conductor (easily) — Why, that's all **right** (handing Alfred the tickets), might happen to **any**body.

A dialogue published in The Wave *of* November 28, 18...

Angelina (fervidly)—Oh! thank you so much. It's very kind of you.

Alfred (loftily, as he pockets the tickets)—I told you, Angelina, that I would fix it somehow.

Angelina—Yes, Alfred, I should have known that I could have relied upon you.

The Conductor—Better hurry up, you'll miss the boat.

Angelina (to the conductor, as she and Alfred move away)—Thank you, again, so *very* much.

Alfred—He *was* a brick after all, wasn't he?

Angelina—He was a *gentleman*, Alfred.

Alfred (turning back)—Wait a minute. I have an idea. (Approaches the conductor and offers him the Isabella Regina.) Have a cigar, sir.

The Conductor—Thanks, I will.

A Miner Interviewed

A SKETCH FROM
The Wave of July 24, 1897.

Mr. Lot O. Goldinsight is in town, recently returned from the Klondyke region, where he has been spending a few weeks of the summer season hunting and fishing. Mr. L. O. Goldinsight reports excellent caribou shooting, and has brought with him a fine stand of horns. The salmon will rise to a fly on the Klondyke, according to the statements of this enthusiastic sportsman, at almost any time during the hot weather. During the intervals of his sport the gentleman employed his time shoveling gold dust into hogsheads.

"It is a very healthy exercise," remarked Mr. Goldinsight, "and especially good for the muscles of the back. I found it tiresome at first, but I assure you that at the end of my stay I could shovel my five hundred pounds per hour and never feel it. Have something to drink?" he added affably. "Won't you sit down?" He removed a flour sack of gold dust from the bottom of an armchair, and the reporter seated himself.

"By the way," said Mr. Goldinsight, "I picked this up in your park to-day. It is really a very curious

A sketch published in The Wave *of* *July* 24, 1897.

specimen; perhaps you can tell me something about it."

He handed the reporter a small round stone, such as is used in gravel walks. The reporter took it in his hand.

"Why, sir," said the reporter, "it is merely a common pebble; we have 'em by the ton down here. It's gravel."

"Really, now," said Mr. Goldinsight, "you surprise me. You know I've been on the Klondyke so long that possibly I might have forgotten. You never see gravel up there, you know. Some prospectors have gone out for it, and I believe one or two specimens have been found near the top of the gold deposits. But the percentage of gravel to gold is so small that I doubt if it will ever pay to mine it extensively. It won't run more than an ounce of gravel to a ton or more of gold."

Mr. Goldinsight carefully returned the pebble to its buckskin bag and locked it in his safe.

"I understand, sir," said the reporter, "that you have a couple of ship-loads of gold dust on the way down."

"Ballast, merely ballast," returned Mr. Goldinsight, airily. "I have an offer from a concrete paving company to whom I expect to dispose of the whole consignment. It is found that the gold dust mixes well with the mortar and sand, and makes a good, firm pavement."

*A sketch
published in*
The Wave *of
July* 24, 1897.

I

Mr. Goldinsight was asked as to whether the finds of gold along the Klondyke would have an effect upon the value of lead.

"It is hardly possible," he assured the reporter. "It might be run into bullets, but the Winchester and Remington, and other firms are using the steel bullets so much of late that there will be practically no competition in that direction. For gas and water pipes—now there might be a market in that direction. But these gravel deposits you speak of down here—"

"Oh, there can be no doubt that the pebbles are here," answered the reporter.

"You don't think that the reports that have reached us along the Klondyke have been exaggerated?"

"Not in the least. You may say that the supply of pebbles along the ocean beach below the Cliff House is practically inexhaustible, and pebbles have been found as far south as Pescadero. There are even indications of pebbles and gravel in the Sierras and along the Mother Lode, but there they are so mixed with gold that they are considered of a low grade."

"When this news reaches the Klondyke," said Mr. Goldinsight, "I assure you there will be a rush for this place. The men there will have the pebble fever at once. The difficulty will be in getting out of Alaska. You know there are two routes—one down the Yukon and one, very dangerous, over Chilly-Cat Pass. However, when a man is picking up pebbles and gravel by the hatful he won't think of his past hardships. You know," continued Mr. Goldinsight, "I am about to incorporate a company."

"Indeed, for what purpose?"

"To mine for gravel hereabouts and transport it to the Klondyke; it would fetch something like 20 cents an ounce there."

"But what would the miners there want with it?"

"Well," said Mr. Lot O. Goldinsight, "it would be a good thing to mix the gravel with our gold in order that we might pan the gold easier."

A sketch published in The Wave *of* *July* 24, 1897.

A drawing by Frank Norris from the University of California Blue and Gold, 1894.

When a Woman Hesitates—A SKETCH *from* 𝕿𝖍𝖊 𝖂𝖆𝖛𝖊 *of May* 29, 1897.

Mrs. Trevor was not at home when Barclay called that afternoon, but the butler had instructions to tell him to wait for her; she had gone—where, Barclay did not quite understand—and would be back in half an hour. Barclay had waited for perhaps five minutes in the drawing-room examining the familiar paintings on the walls and turning idly the leaves of the gift books on the table, when a rustle of skirts from the direction of the portieres made him start and face about quickly, with the idea in his mind that Mrs. Trevor had returned sooner than expected. But it was not Mrs. Trevor who stood smiling at him in the door. Instead it was a very pretty—a wonderfully pretty— young girl of twenty or thereabouts, dressed in a smart tea-gown that set her off admirably.

"Oh," she said, with a mixture of coquetry and timidity that was charming, "is this—this is Mr. Barclay, I believe?"

Barclay replied that he had every reason to think it was.

"I am Miss Willis," she went on; "Mrs. Trevor's cousin."

Barclay bowed.

A sketch published in The Wave *of* May 29, 1897.

"From the country."

Barclay smiled, because it was evident she expected him to.

"And Mrs. Trevor asked me to—to talk to you in case you came before she got back—and—and—I don't think she will be back for half an hour."

"It is delightful!" murmured Barclay, vaguely.

"Which?" said Miss Willis, beginning to laugh. "By the way, you had better sit down." She settled herself upon the sofa.

"Why, just this." Barclay waved his hand as though to take in the situation, inclusive of Miss Willis and himself.

"It's delicious!" said Miss Willis.

Barclay sat down—upon the sofa.

"But we've not been introduced, you know," began Miss Willis, shaking her head at him.

"We must get along without it."

"Do you think we can?"

"Can what?"

"Get along—together."

"Some one has said that 'together' is the prettiest word in the language. Yes, I think we can."

"But will you meet me half way—you know, I'm from the country."

*A sketch
published in
The Wave of
May 29, 1897.*

"I'll do more than that, if you will let me." Barclay dropped his hand upon the sofa.

"That would be very kind. Oh, I was to make tea for you, so Mrs. Trevor said."

"Oh, bother the tea! Wouldn't you rather talk?"

"I think I would—to you."

Barclay looked quizzically at the point of his varnished boot.

"You know, I—I'm not in such a hurry to have Mrs. Trevor come home." He slid his hand an inch or two along the sofa.

"And she won't be here for—a—whole—half—hour."

"I've heard of a battle that was won in less than that time. Do you think a girl could be?"

"Could be won in half an hour?"

"Yes."

"That would depend much upon the man, wouldn't it?"

"If the girl would meet him half way?"

"But one man promised to do more than that."

"I say, Miss Willis——"

"If the girl would let him, you know. And she might not let him——"

Barclay's hand paused.

"Unless——"

It moved forward again.

"Unless she felt sure the man thought she was worth the battle."

The hand moved forward another inch. There was an instant's silence, then Barclay said:

"She is worth it, I think."

"But it might be a long and very dreadful battle."

"I'm thinking of the girl, not of that." As he spoke his hand touched hers, in the folds of her gown. He took it in his own. She did not move. Suddenly she flashed a smile at him.

"I'm sorry Mrs. Trevor keeps you waiting so long. It's more than half an hour already."

"I'm not."

"Are you quite sure of that?"

"Absolutely."

Miss Willis drew her hand from his and rose to her feet with a good-humored smile, then she said:

"I ought not to be surprised at her being late, because I know that she does not intend to come at all."

"Not coming at all?" said Barclay, puzzled.

"No."

"What do you mean?"

"I mean that Mrs. Trevor has digged a little pit for you, and that you have fallen into the midst of it."

"The deuce!" exclaimed Barclay, his eyes widening.

"You know—or perhaps you don't know," continued Miss Willis, smiling good-naturedly, "that Mrs. Trevor has been of late a little—just a little—suspicious of your protestations of devotion. She thinks that you are a sad rogue, Mr. Barclay, and that despite your

A sketch published in The Wave of May 29, 1897.

*A sketch
published in
The Wave of
May 29, 1897.*

assurances, that you would flirt most outrageously, most unconscionably, with the first pretty girl who would permit it."

"Come, now, I say, Miss Willis."

"And so, since Mrs. Trevor has the great goodness to think me not too unpresentable, she asked me to receive you this afternoon, and to make myself agreeable, in order that I might inform her afterward as to results."

"The devil she did!" cried Barclay, quite out of countenance. He got to his feet, his forehead puckering uneasily.

"She even went so far," said Miss Willis, always with the same entrancing smile, "as to confide to me two little notes, one of which I was to hand you in case you proved faithful, and the other should you prove false. In one of them—the one you would have received had you been good—she thanks you for your constancy, and swears to you that she will always and forever love you; the other one—well, the other one treats you in the manner you have deserved and gives you your freedom."

"And naturally," said Barclay, gloomily, "it is this last one you are going to give me?"

"Don't you think you have merited it?"

"How do you know one letter from the other?"

"The bad one I marked with a cross—see?" and she held it towards him.

A sketch published in The Wave of May 29, 1897.

"I say—look here, Miss Willis," exclaimed Barclay, suddenly; "are you vexed with me for what has happened this afternoon? Do you regret our little tete-a-tete?"

Miss Willis put her lips together and turned the note about and about in her fingers. She said nothing.

"Well, then," said Barclay, "when you tell Mrs. Trevor all about it, she won't be very well pleased will she, now?"

"Probably not."

"Women like Mrs. Trevor, even when they are expecting it, don't like to be—deceived."

"She will be furious."

"Especially when their successful rival is their little cousin—from the country?"

"That is one way of looking at it, of course."

"Which you hadn't thought of. I shall be dismissed, of course: but aren't you afraid she will send you home as well? You know the 'woman scorned' quotation?"

"She might send me back—that is quite true."

"Whereas, if you should give me the other letter—the one without the cross—Mrs. Trevor will never know, and I can come often, and—and—and have you make tea for me when Mrs. Trevor is out, and thus you and I and Mrs. Trevor—all of us, in fact—will be happy. Now what do you say?"

Miss Willis hesitated a moment. (You know what

When a Woman Hesitates

A sketch
published in
The Wave of
May 29, 1897.

happens when a woman hesitates.) Her eyes met Barclay's, and she smiled in spite of herself.

Then without a word she handed him the unmarked letter.

There was a roll of wheels on the asphalt outside, and the clapping of a carriage door.

"There is Mrs. Trevor now!" exclaimed Miss Willis.

"JUSTIN STURGIS"

A drawing by
Frank Norris from
the University of
California
Blue and Gold,
1894.

Western City Types ✍

A SERIES OF SKETCHES FROM
The Wave *of* May 2-16, 1896.

I. *The Plumber's Apprentice*

His name is "Jonesee," and he is a tinner and gas-fitter during six days of the week, or at least attempts to persuade his brother-in-law, into whose shop he has been received, that such is his serious occupation. Jonesee tried to impress the fiction upon himself during the first days of his apprenticeship, but the strain of sustaining the character increased in proportion as the novelty of the work diminished, until he has come by gentle degrees to keeping up appearances only during the times when the boss is in, and they are literally "appearances" even then. He never works unless he is absolutely driven to it, and he probably never will as long as he can live at home and exploit his father—who is an annealer in the Mint—for enough change to keep him in beer and "cigareets."

In the back room of the grimy tin-shop on Polk Street, Jonesee languishes and chafes by turns. The only ornaments on the walls are a couple of pictures cut from bill posters of the "Danites," and a dirty map of San Francisco, on which the location of the

Published in
The Wave *of*
May 2, 1896.

*A sketch
published in
The Wave of
May 2, 1896.*

tin-shop is at once betrayed by a worn and soiled spot, the result of frequent contact with greasy finger-tips. Jonesee hates the place, and is much more content when he is sent out to do an odd job in the neighborhood.

At such times one sees him on the front platforms of cable cars, his hand-furnace for heating his soldering irons between his feet, together with his solder-sticks, pliers, clamping tools, etc., wrapped in their carpet case, his pockets loaded with brass faucets, short sections of lead pipe, and tweezers.

On these occasions he wears a suit that has once been black, but has now faded to a shade of green, except upon the trousers above the knee, where, by constant friction with lead and grease and dirt, they are thickly coated with a glazed and shining varnish of black. His battered derby hat is of a blackish green as well, and is marked with sweat stains around the band. He is always smoking the butt of a "cigareet," which sticks to his lower lip even when he opens his mouth to talk.

He is even more contented when he goes out to lunch at noon in the Polk-street restaurant, in the window of which one sees three china pigs and a plaster of Paris cow knee-deep in a thick layer of white beans. He likes to gabble and lounge at length among the postmen, car-conductors, and barbers who frequent the place, and hear the latest word on ward politics and prize-fights, or shake dice or match nickels for cigars.

Sunday, however, is Jonesee's great day. It is the one day of the seven when he is released from the work of seeming to work. He is not in evidence till the afternoon. Then sometimes he goes out to the Park or to the Cliff House, or sometimes, on rare occasions, rents a horse and buggy with a friend and *drives* there; sometimes he goes "across the Bay" on a public picnic, or sometimes "takes in" the races, or balloon jumps or high dives as opportunity affords.

But his favorite and characteristic occupation of a Sunday afternoon is general and promiscuous loafing, posing, trying to be tough, showing himself off in his cheap finery, for at such times he is dressed with scrupulous attention.

His soft felt hat is pushed back upon his head far enough to show his hair parted very much to one side, neatly oiled and plastered and brought down over his temple in a beautiful flat curve. He wears an inexpensive "Prince Albert" invariably unbuttoned to show the flowered design of his waistcoat. In the lapel of this coat he wears a tuberose. His stand-up collar is very low and overlaps in front, while around this collar and often getting above it is a crocheted four-in-hand "necktie" of salmon pink silk, tied very tightly and transfixed with a scarfpin representing a palette and brushes, with four colors in variously tinted

A sketch published in The Wave *of May 2, 1896.*

*A sketch
published in
The Wave of
May 2, 1896.*

Rhinestones. He fastens this necktie to the side of his shirt so that it traverses *diagonally* the whole of the triangular expanse left by the vest. His trousers fit him very tightly and are of light brown cloth with broad chocolate colored stripes. The cuffs around his thick red wrists are frayed and in one of his freckled fists he carries a cane, a slender wisp of ebony with a gold head, won at the Tinners' and Gasfitters' Prize Masquerade Ball.

Thus arrayed, and attended by odors of tobacco, beer, hair oil, and German cologne, he lounges with three or four others of his stripe about the entrances of corner groceries, where a Milwaukee beer sign decorates the salient corner and where you may see displayed advertisements for cheap butter, eggs, and tea, painted in green marking ink upon wrapping paper. Here, together with his friends, he will while the time away, talking loud, swearing, spitting, scuffling, and joshing the girls that pass in twos and threes. Now and then he and his friends will go into the bar behind the store and have a "steam" or sometimes himself and a comrade will take off their coats, go into the middle of the street and with frequent cries of "all de way now" pitch curves at one another with an adamantine ball. Toward the close of the afternoon he will sometimes go with them to Golden Gate Avenue and watch the "turn-outs" coming home from the park, commenting upon the horses, and joshing the girl bicyclists. In the evening he goes to a cheap theater, and occasionally closes the day's enjoyment by becoming drunk and disorderly.

II. *The "Fast Girl"*

She dresses in a black, close-fitting bolero jacket of imitation astrachan with enormous leg-of-mutton sleeves of black velvet, a striped silk skirt, and a very broad hat, tilted to one side. Her hair is very blonde, though, somehow, coarse and dry, and a little flat curl of it lies low over her forehead. She is marvelously pretty.

She belongs to a certain class of young girl that is very common in the city. She is what men, amongst each other, call "gay," though that is the worst that can be said of her. She is virtuous, but the very fact that it is necessary to say so is enough to cause the statement to be doubted.

When she was younger and a pupil at the Girls' High School, she had known, and had even been the companion of, girls of good family, but since that time these girls have come to ignore her. Now almost all of her acquaintances are men, and to most of these she has never been introduced. They have managed to get acquainted with her on Kearny Street, at the theaters, at the Mechanics' Fair, and at baseball games. She tells these men that her name is "Ida."

A sketch published in The Wave *of May 9, 1896.*

A sketch published in The Wave of May 9, 1896.

The "Fast" Girl

She loves to have a "gay time" with them, which, for her, means to drink California champagne, to smoke cigarettes, and to kick at the chandelier. Understand distinctly, however, that she is not "bad," that there is nothing vicious about her. Ida is too clever to be "bad," and is as morbidly careful of appearances and as jealous of her reputation as only fast girls can be.

She lives with her people on Golden Gate Avenue. Her father has a three-fourths interest in a carpet-cleaning "establishment" in the Mission, and her mother gives lessons in hand-painting on china and on velvet.

In the evening, especially if it be a Saturday evening, Ida invents all sorts of excuses to go "down town." You see her then on Kearny or Market streets about the time the theaters open, arm in arm with one or perhaps two other girls who are precisely like her. At this time she is not in the least "loud," either in dress or in conversation, but somehow when she is in the street she cannot raise a finger or open her mouth without attracting attention.

Like "Jonesee," Sunday is her great day. Ida usually spends it "Across the Bay" somewhere. A party is gotten up and there is no "chaperon." Two or three of the men with whom she and her friends have become acquainted during the week arrange the "date." The day's amusement is made to include a lunch at one of the suburban hotels and a long drive in a hired

A sketch published in The Wave *of May 9, 1896.*

"rig." The party returns home on one of the ferry boats late in the afternoon. By that time they are quite talked out, their good spirits are gone, and they sit in a row, side by side, exchanging monosyllables. Ida's face is red, her hair is loose, and the little blonde curl has lost its crispness. She has taken off her gloves by this time. In one of her bare hands she carries her escort's cane, and in the other a bunch of wilted wild flowers. Sometimes, however, the party returns to the city in a later boat, one that makes the trip after dark. Then everything is changed. The party "pairs off" at once. You will see Ida and her "fellar" sitting in one of the dark corners of the deck. The fellar sits as close as the length of his acquaintance with Ida will justify. He rests his elbow on the rail back of her and, by and by, carelessly lets his forearm drop at full length.

When the Mechanics' Fair opens Ida rarely misses an evening. I remember that I once saw her and the fellar in the art gallery up-stairs. Ida's mother, "who gives lessons in hand-painting," had an exhibit there which they were interested to find: a bunch of yellow poppies painted on black velvet and framed in gilt. When they had found it they stood before it some little time hazarding their opinions and then moved on from one picture to another. Ida had the fellar buy a catalogue and made it a duty to find the title of every picture, for she professes to be very fond of

*A sketch
published in
The Wave of
May 9, 1896.*

hand-painting. She had "taken it up" at one time and abandoned it only because the oil or the turpentine or something had been unhealthy for her.

On this occasion she looked at each picture carefully, her head on one side. "Of course," she explained to the fellar, "I'm no critic, I only know what I like. I like those 'heads,' those ideal heads like that one," and she pointed with her arm outstretched to a picture of the head of a young girl with disheveled brown hair and upturned eyes. The title of the picture was "Faith."

"Yes," said Ida, reflectively, "I like that kind."

III. *An Art Student*

*A sketch
published in
The Wave of
May 16, 1896.*

He is in evidence to the world outside, at the opening days of spring exhibits, and in and about the art gallery in the Mechanics' Fair. Sometimes you see him coming back to the city on one of the ferry boats late Wednesday and Saturday afternoons. He has been sketching over in Alameda or among the Berkeley hills. He carries his stretchers, camp-stool, umbrella, and paint-box in a clumsy shawl-strapped bundle, and his empty lunch-basket is full of faded eschscholtzias and wild flowers.

On week days he works—and he works hard—at the School of Design—the Art Institute. For the past five years he has been working away here desperately,

A sketch published in The Wave *of May* 16, 1896.

painting carrots, dead fish, bunches of onions, and, above all, stone jugs. He toils at these jugs with infinite pains. If he can manage to reproduce truthfully the little film of dust that gathers upon them, he is happy. A dusty stone jug is his ideal in life.

He thinks he is an artist and he is quite conscientious about it, and thoroughly believes himself capable of passing opinions upon any picture painted. He expresses these opinions in a loud voice before the picture in question, looking at it with half-shut eyes, making vague gestures at it with his closed fist, moving the thumb as though it were a brush.

Once in a while you see his pictures—still life "studies" of stone jugs and bunches of onions—in the exhibits. Occasionally these are noticed in the local papers. He cuts out these notices and carefully pastes them in his scrap-book, which he leaves about in conspicuous places in his studio.

And his studio. His studio is his room at home (he lives with his people). He tries to hide the stationary wash-stand behind screens and hangings, and he softens the rigidity of the white marble mantelpiece by hanging a yellow "drape" upon one corner. The room is dirty and cluttered; studies of dusty stone jugs are pinned or tacked upon the walls; flattened paint tubes lie about the window-sills, and there is a strangling odor of turpentine and fixative in the air that mingles with the smell of tobacco and the odor of cooking food from the kitchen down-stairs.

An Art Student

A sketch published in The Wave *of May* 16, 1896.

Art with him is *paint*. He condescends to no other medium than oil and colored earths. Bouguereau is his enthusiasm; he can rise no higher than that, and he looks down with an amused smile upon the illustrators, the pen-and-ink men, Gibson, Smedley, Remmington, and the rest. "Good in their way, oh, yes, but Gibson is very superficial, you know." He is given to astonishing you in this way. Pictures that you admire he damns with a phrase; those you believe to be execrable, he enthuses over.

He believes himself to be Bohemian, but by Bohemianism he understands merely the wearing of large soft felt hats and large bow scarfs and the drinking of beer in German "resorts." His Bohemianism is not dangerous.

What becomes of the "Art" student, I have often wondered. He starts early at his work. Even at the High School he covers the fly-leaves of all his books with pictures, and carves the head of the principal in chalk. At home he has made fearful copies of the sentimental pictures in the "Home Book of Art." His parents are astonished, become vaguely ambitious, and send him to the Art School before he has hardly begun his education. Here, as I have told you, he toils away the best years of his life over "still life" studies, enthusiastic over little things, very ambitious in small ways. A year passes, two years, then five, six and ten, he is still working as hard as ever, and he is nearly a middle aged man now. You meet him on his way home in the evening and he takes you to supper and shows you his latest "piece." It is a study of turnips and onions, grouped about a dusty, stone jug.

He never sells a picture. He has given his life to his work. He grows older; he tries to make his "art" pay. He drifts into decorative art; is employed perhaps as a clerk in an art store. If he's lucky he is taken on a newspaper and does the pen-and-ink work that he once affected to despise. He's over thirty by this time, and is what he will be for the rest of his life. All his ambitions are vanished, his enthusiasm's dead, but little by little he comes to be quite contented.

A sketch published in The Wave *of May* 16, 1896.

The Opinions of Leander SKETCHES FROM
The Wave of July-August, 1897.

I. 'Holdeth forth upon our boys and the ways of them

Published in The Wave *of July 24, 1897.*

I was villifying the head waiter in The Drinkand the other night, just after the play, because he would not let me sit in the main room where the orchestra plays, when Leander came up.

"Come on, Just," said he; "you know they won't let you sit in here unless you are with ladies."

"We wouldn't permit a lady to sit in here unless she was with a gentleman, sir," interposed the autocrat.

"The danger," said I, "is due, I should suppose, to the mingling of the sexes, not to their separation—divided we stand, united we fall. You will, perhaps, recall the fable of Æsop, of the two jars floating in a cistern—*Haec fabula docet* that——"

The autocrat wavered at this point.

"I observe," said I, pressing home, "a vacant table near the door with two places——"

*A sketch
published in
The Wave of
July 24, 1897*

"Well, you know," protested the autocrat, feebly, "it's against all regulation."

We sat down.

Leander began to bow to people he knew who were sitting at near-by tables. The place glittered with electricity and silverware. There was a staccato note of conversation in the air. The orchestra sobbed away at La Paloma.

"Perfect! Perfect!" murmured Leander under his breath.

"Theatre?" I asked, and looked at his clothes.

"No—call."

"What! in a brown tweed suit, tan shoes, and a blue shirt with a white collar?"

"Thanks for the collar. Yes, I have been making a call."

"In a sack suit? Good Lord!"

"Remember this is San Francisco—1897!"

"True! true! But the suit is not even black, nor the shoes—really, Leander."

"I know her rather well."

"Still——"

"My boy (I am Leander's senior by six years), you come from a place near Brooklyn, called New York, where everybody must conform to a certain mold in clothes as well as ideas. We in the freer West avons change tout cela. Out here a man does not always have to appear in evening dress after six, nor even

A sketch published in The Wave *of July 24, 1897.*

|

wear a high hat of a Sunday afternoon, unless he wants to."

We ordered our drinks. Leander, I think, had an oyster cocktail. After a moment's reflection he looked about the place, and exclaimed, nodding his head:

"For the young man with a small salary, who lives at home, San Francisco is the best place in the world."

"Or the worst," I observed.

"Huh!" exclaimed Leander, "there's something in that. But it charms you."

"So does a snake," I added, sepulchrally, "only to bite and poison you afterward."

"I say! I say!" exclaimed Leander, looking at me in some alarm; "what's up—been bitten?"

"Not yet—only charmed."

"Say, Just," exclaimed Leander, "last week we said something about the girls out here. How about 'Our Boys?' We—I mean you and I, and all the rest of us—are we desirable—are we very particularly fine?"

"We are," said I, "what our English cousins would call a jolly rum lot."

"Perhaps not quite as bad as that. But we're not very nice."

"Let's see—how aren't we nice?"

"We lack purpose, aim, ambition. We are content with little things—little glasses of liqueur, for instance" (this significantly; I was drinking a creme de menthe myself). "We do not rise to the dignity of

A sketch published in The Wave *of July* 24, 1897.

champagne, or even to the height of straight Bourbon. Life," began Leander, rhetorically, "life in this city of ours is like a little glasslet of liqueur—pungent, sweet, heady, but without foundation, without stability—an appetizer that creates only small desires, easily gratified, and we are content with those. We are like this, we men—you and I and the rest of the fellows—at our best."

"Heavens! What must we be at our worst?"

"At our worst," said Leander, severely, "we get drunk and come to dances that way."

"Come, now——"

"Hoh! My dear fellow, it's a common sight."

"A fellow under the influence——"

"No, drunk—I choose to call it drunk."

"At a dance?"

"Worse—dancing."

"With a girl?"

"Whom, perhaps, you know and admire."

"Why not punch his head on the spot?"

"Bad form, head-punching, at a function."

"But not drunkenness?"

Leander shrugged.

"Who are they—what class do they trot in, in Heaven's name?"

"Ours. Many of them are college chaps in their junior and senior years."

"Little fools."

A sketch published in The Wave *of July 24, 1897.*

On our Boys

"Hear! Hear! and some even among the older men; but it's mostly the younger boys. Now, when these boys grow up and begin to associate with the kind of girl we were talking about last week—the kind of girl who smokes a cigarette on the sly and drinks a cocktail—then——"

"Leander, spare me the picture! After us the deluge."

"There's one of them now. Look at the third table."

"The slender chap with the pinkish eyelids and the impossible tie?"

"Sure! I know him—he's a Junior at Berkeley. That's his fifth pousse cafe."

"Little beast."

"He's drunk already, and I saw him just like that on a yachting party last Thursday, when there were a lot of nice girls along."

"Faugh!"

"And everybody knew it, and the girls—some of them—said, 'Oh, well, you know it's only little Jack Spratt.'"

"And yet we would call that a gentleman out here."

"As Doctor Pow Len says in Mr. Powers' admirable little play, 'such is the lamentable fact.'"

"A gentleman, that."

"In New York we would tell him his carriage was ready."

"Here he's received and called good form."

"I say, Leander, who is that broad-shouldered chap

A sketch published in The Wave *of July* 24, 1897.

behind him, sitting with his back towards us? He's got a good pair of shoulders on him, and I don't think his tailor is responsible for 'em, either."

"Rather well put up, to be sure. Oh, I say, Just, look what he's ordered."

"Well, I declare! Tea and toast and a little fruit! Now, imagine a chap asking for tea and toast and a little fruit in The Drinkand! What a jay! Say, Leander, I think he must be a Christian Endeavorer who's blown into the wrong place."

"I've seen that chap somewhere, though," said Leander, perplexedly; "wonder where it could have been?"

"Hoh! Tea and toast and a little fruit! What a dead farmer—and—there! he's just declined to smoke. Poor little dear—if his mamma could only see him now! Bet he's got a C. E. badge on as long as your arm."

"Where in snakes," muttered Leander, "have I seen those shoulders and that head? Wish he'd turn around."

"There—he's getting up."

The tea and toast chap turned about, and we saw his face. Leander uttered an exclamation:

"It's Spider Kelly, the prize-fighter."

"Nonsense! Would he take tea and toast?—he——"

"Training, y'know. Fights Lon Agnew next week. Ten rounds, with a decision."

*A sketch
published in
The Wave of
July 24, 1897.*

"Leander—let's take a walk. I'll pay for the drinks."

"You'd better."

There was a long silence after this, then Leander said:

"Anyhow, I've more respect just at this moment for the Spider than I have for the little college chap."

"At least he has a purpose, even if he is not 'good form,'" I murmured.

And with that we went away.

"JUSTIN STURGIS"

II. 'Commenteth at length upon letters received

*A sketch
published in
The Wave of
July 31, 1897.*

Last Tuesday afternoon I went around to my favorite Chinese restaurant—the one on the top floor, of the See Yup silk-merchant's, that overlooks the Plaza. I have lately contracted the habit of betaking myself thitherward for an afternoon cup of tea and a quiet half hour with a book and a cigar. It ought to be cigarettes, but I've promised a girl that— I mean that it's very charming in this golden balcony, tea is never so delicious as it is here, and your book never so interesting, and your cigar—cigar, I say, mark you—never so delicious. I like to go to this place alone, for I feel it is mine by right of discovery, but on Tuesday last I caromed against Leander at

A sketch published in The Wave *of July* 31, 1897.

the street corner. He was in Chinatown for Heaven knows what purpose. Of course I had to take him along.

"I say, Just," he remarked, as he sat down on a teak-wood stool and plucked up his trousers at the knee; "I say, old man, this is completely out of sight. Say, Just, wouldn't this be a great place to bring the One Particular Girl to?"

I said something or other here.

Leander grinned with bland incredulity, then added: "Would it be good form, now?" Then suddenly: "Apropos of that, Just, you and your good form and your bad form and your confounded 'opinions' have brought me into trouble."

"Oh, get out!"

"I won't—they have!"

"I've been getting letters."

"Well?"

"From girls—girls that I don't know—who——"

"Well, there's the police, you know. The law will protect you."

"Oh, shut up! Wait till I finish. I've been getting letters from girls, and they—and they—well, they say things."

"It's a habit girls have. What do they say?"

"Here," said Leander, gravely unfolding a sheet, "is one of them. Read it."

I took the letter in his hands.

A sketch published in The Wave *of July* 31, 1897.

|

"Hum!" said I; "unglazed paper, and ruled at that! Mph! Reeks of sachet, too!"

"Oh, never mind that; it's what she says."

"Mr. Leander—Dear Sir: I read with great attention your strictures upon the young ladies of San Francisco Society ('spells it with a big S,' I commented) and I wish to take this opportunity of refuting and denying your unmanly ('say, that's rough!') and malicious charges. The young ladies of this city," I continued, "are as well bred and refined as any of the world, and though I have been in Society for over ten years ('that's a give-away!' I cried, and, I'm afraid, I cackled) and I have never seen the slightest approach to any of the practices ('practices! Good Lord!') to which you are pleased to allude with such shameful publicity ('Oh, well, she's a chaperone—you can see that with one hand tied behind you.') In closing, all I can say is that you and your frivolous friend——"

"That's you, Just!" exclaimed Leander, grimly.

"——must have been associated with a very peculiar ('peculiar, underscored') kind of young women. You should not, I scarcely need remind you, judge all other ladies according to their own somewhat limited experiences." No signature.

"Well!" said Leander.

"Well!" said I.

"What did you get me into this thing for?" com-

*A sketch
published in
The Wave of
July* 31, 1897.

plained Leander; "do you think I like getting that kind of a letter?"

"No," said I, "I shouldn't think you would."

"Well, then, what the devil——"

Leander's voice rose to a shrill wail.

"Leander, there's nothing heroic about you. You are not willing to suffer in a good cause. You want to do all the hitting, and when someone—someone who's been ten years in society—hits back, you squeal. Shame on you! Now, I, too, have received a letter," said I, proudly; "in fact, several of them on this same subject."

"You have?" cried Leander, blankly; "let's hear 'em."

"No, one will do; they're much alike."

"Much like mine?"

"Much unlike," I returned, loftily. "Observe now," (I held the letter towards him) "pale blue paper, rather heavy, and suggestive of parchment—very faint odor of heliotrope—and, you see, she had a monogram, because, you notice, she has cut it out to conceal her identity."

"Let's hear what she has to say."

"Dear Mr. Sturgis—" I read.

"That's better than Mr. Leander — Dear Sir," moaned Leander.

"I should say so," said I, very proudly. "Dear Mr. Sturgis: I read your article last Saturday on 'Girls,'

A sketch
published in
The Wave of
July 31, 1897.

On Letters Received

and I think if more people had the sense to write similar articles, it might do the San Francisco girl some good."

"Huh!" said I, breaking off; "your girl said it was an unmanly and malicious charge."

"She wasn't young, I'll bet a hat," grumbled Leander; "and her paper was ruled—go on."

I went on: "——some good, and open their eyes to what men really think of them——"

"But we think very well of them," cried Leander; "that's just why we deplore their—their—vagaries."

"——they think it's funny and that the men laugh, but indeed they don't. I am one of the girls that are 'out,' but believe me, we are not all that way."

"Hear! Hear!" cried Leander, pounding with his stick.

"——and those of us that have——"

"She will use 'that' for 'who'; but never mind."

"——that have some sense of refinement feel just as the men do. Although I do not sign my name, I know you and you know me quite well."

"There!" said I, putting back the letter; "what do you say to that?"

"Corking fine little girl," commented Leander; "wish she'd written to me. May be, though, she comes from Oakland."

"No; she bought this paper at Robertson's. It's stamped on the flap of the envelope."

*A sketch
published in
The Wave of
July* 31, 189?.

Leander drank off the rest of his tea, and chewed a pickled watermelon rind thoughtfully. Then:

"Just," said he, "who's to blame?"

"Who's to blame for what?"

"Who's to blame for the whole blooming show. Why do the girls smoke cigarettes and drink cocktails on the sly, and why do men come to functions drunk?"

"Leander, this brutal frankness——"

"Well, call it the vagaries of the younger set, if you like. Are the men at fault, or the girls, or is it the chaperons, or is it — by Jove, we have never thought of that!—is it the girls' mothers?"

"There's one thing," said I, "that's certain; the girls wouldn't smoke if they didn't think the men found it amusing."

"But that's just it," cried Leander. "The men don't. The girls don't know—they don't believe that the very men who encourage them to smoke have a sort of secret contempt for them after all."

"But they say they like a girl better because she's daring and chic and independent of convention. They call her fin-de-siecle and all that."

"Yes, that's what they tell the girl. But amongst ourselves, now, did you ever, in all your life, hear one man tell another that he liked to see a girl smoke, or that he liked her better because she knew to handle a cigarette?"

I reflected. I tried to remember one—I am still trying.

*A sketch
published in*
The Wave *of
July* 31, 1897.

"No, you never did, and more than that, the girls only know what the man says to them. He says, 'Oh, go on; what's a cigarette? Pshaw! I like to see a girl do everything a man does. I like to see a girl up to date.' But we—you and I and the rest of the fellows—know what these same men say of such girls among ourselves. They 'Hoh, yes; that little girl;' then they shrug one shoulder and smile a bit out of one side of their mouth (you know the meaning of that!); 'yes, that little girl,' they say, 'she's gay all right. You can have the hell of a good time with her.' I wonder what the girl would say if she could see and hear him? I wonder if she'd think it was so damned funny to smoke a cigarette then? Admit that I'm right, now. Say, ain't I right?"

"Well, I guess you are, Leander. But now look here: You say the girls would stop smoking if they knew how the men talked about 'em?"

"Of course. Do you suppose a girl likes to smoke?"

"Well, now, listen here. These men that come to functions drunk—here's a question for you—do the girls think less of them for it? How do the girls talk about them when they are among themselves?"

"That's a point to be considered," said Leander, as we rose to go.

"JUSTIN STURGIS"

III. *'Falleth from grace and subsequently from a springboard*

A sketch published in The Wave *of August* 7, 1897.

The other morning I went, rather early, to the "Lure-you-in" Baths for my accustomed plunge. It is really very pleasant to take a swim and a subsequent cup of coffee in this fashion before breakfast. There are but few in the baths at that hour, and the water is almost as fresh as at the beach. As I was coming out I bumped against Leander, who was just going in, dressed in a suit of pale salmon-pink, nearly flesh-colored, and quite flesh tight.

"Neptune rising from the waves," he exclaimed, with a grin.

"Venus going to the bath," I retaliated, staring significantly at his wondrous costume.

"Come, now—I say—really, you know," he exclaimed, all in a breath.

"Wake up!" said I, "it's morning." At this, just as the heroine does in novels, he started and passed his hand over his brow.

"I'm a bit absent-minded this morning," he pleaded.

"Huh!" I snorted; "I've often noticed that absence of mind."

Then Leander said two bad words, and I was fain to punch his head. After this (some time after) we sat down on the end of the springboard, and Leander unburdened himself of his trouble.

A sketch
published in
The Wave of
August 7, 1897.

"Well," says he, "you see, it was like this——"

"There were two of us," I interrupted, "and the other was a girl."

"Well, as we were saying," began Leander, "I called on this girl the other night, and——"

"Wait a minute. How well did you know her?"

"One dance, one tea, two functions, and a call."

"Oh, intimately, then. Remember, this is San Francisco. First name?"

"Yep—at the tea."

"Yours too?"

"Of course."

"Fancy calling a man 'Leander'!"

"Shut up—she says 'Lee.'"

"Idyllic! and her's—what's her's?"

Leander drew himself up.

"Mr. Sturgis!" frostily.

But Leander could not be effective in that bathing-suit and with those dangling calves. Yet I apologized.

"I don't want to know her confounded name, then." said I; "but I thought you did not approve of this sort of thing, this—this—this too easy familiarity?"

"No more I do. But I told you I was in trouble."

"It seems to me we don't get far along in this story."

"Well, I called on this girl."

"You've said that three times. Did she let the maid open the door?"

"No, she opened it herself."

A sketch published in The Wave *of* August 7, 1897.

"I thought so. Well, now, we're inside the house. Do we go into the parlor?"

"Nope—small reception-room at back, one lamp, one chair——"

"What?"

"Wait till I finish—one sofa——"

"Ah, sofa!"

"One——"

"The rest of the inventory is immaterial, irrelevant, and incompetent. The stage is set for a drama. Was it comedy?"

"Tragedy!" said Leander in sepulchral tones.

"One thing more—had the girl come 'out'?"

"She had—rather far. However, her 'position is assured.'"

"Hum! But aren't you rather caddish, Leander, to tell me all this?"

"You don't know but what I'm lying."

"I had forgotten that contingency."

"And if it doesn't apply to one case it applies to another?"

"True. Vorwartz!"

"Well, I shook hands with her, and——"

"Held her hand?"

"Um-hum."

"How long?"

"For twenty heart-beats," grinned Leander.

"Oh, a couple of seconds, then?"

*A sketch
published in
The Wave of
August 7, 1897.*

"No; 'heart hadn't had time to get started that fast just yet." Say ten seconds. Then she sat down on the sofa, and I took a seat——"

"Where?"

"I say I took a seat."

"Where?"

"Well, I took a seat."

"On the chair?"

"Well—no."

"You said there was one chair in that small reception-room, and the sofa?"

"Um-hum."

"Get on with the story."

"That's what I did with the girl—famously."

"Let's see—the two of you are now sitting on the sofa. The girl is on which side of you?"

"Left."

"Hum! Leander, where is your left elbow?"

Leander grinned.

"It is resting on the back of the sofa, and I am holding my head with my left hand."

"Of course—and then?"

"Then—if ye have tears, prepare to shed them now—then the lamp began to go out."

I gasped.

"I offered," continued Leander, "to turn on the current, but she——"

"Said she loved to sit in the twilight."

A sketch
published in
The Wave of
August 7, 1897.

"Now, how did you know that?"

"Guessed it."

"So we sat——"

"On the sofa."

"In the twilight."

"With your elbow on the back of the sofa; then?"

"Well, then, after a while I—I (Leander coughed slightly and crossed his legs) I let my left hand fall, straight.

"Along the sofa-back?"

"Yes."

"Behind the girl?"

"And she?"

"Never noticed—pretended not to, I mean—and then I moved an eighth of an inch closer, and—well, it was twilight and she was pretty and never noticed —and—and—then—I don't know how it happened, but somehow—confound it, you know the blooming lamp was out and a fellow's only a man, y'know, after all, and I—so I—well, I——"

"Leander," said I, in hollow tones, "Leander, you— kissed—that—girl!"

Leander covered his face with his hands.

"Well, that's a sad case," said I. Leander became animated at once.

"Hoh! You think that's all. The worst is yet to come."

I made as if to fly. Leander caught and pulled me down.

A sketch published in The Wave *of August* 7, 1897.

/

"You misunderstand," he said, severely; "what do you suppose the girl did?"

"Pretended not to notice," I suggested.

"No," wailed Leander; "no, no! she jumped up as if worked by a spring, an' shook all over an' began to cry. I say, she did, an' said I was no gentleman, an' how dared I take such a liberty with her, an' no man had ever kissed her before, an' wasn't I ashamed of myself, an'-I-don't-know-what-all-else. Yes, she did, and there I sat like a lump on a log, an'—well, that's all, an' I've felt as cheap as six bits ever since. Oh, Lord! what a fool a man is! That I should make such a break—I—I" (he smote his salmon-pink breast) "I of all men who have preached—but this settles it for good and all."

"Here endeth the first lesson," said I. "But the girl was to blame. She's no one to thank but herself. You needn't cut up rough, Leander."

"The girl!" said Leander, blankly.

"Think it over now. This was only your second call. She allowed you to treat her with a certain amount of familiarity, opened the door for you herself, saw you alone and not in the parlor, called you—good Lord!— called you 'Leander'!"

"Lee," murmured Leander.

"——let you use her first name, let you hold her hand, never stopped or discouraged your little advances from chair to sofa, and from sofa to sofa-

A sketch published in The Wave *of August* 7, 1897.

back, and so on; gave you every reason to suppose that you might kiss her without fear and without reproach, and then, when you had——"

"It was awful the way she went on—actually cried!"

"I'm not in the least sorry for her. She was entirely to blame. You were just a beastly natural-born man, acting according to your lights. I'm afraid even the best of us, under similar circumstances——"

"Why, what a muff you'd be not to," shouted Leander.

"All good girls draw their line somewhere, only some draw it later than others—this girl drew her's too late."

"When should she have drawn it, or where?"

"Between the chair and that sofa."

There was a pause:

"Look here," exclaimed Leander, turning upon me fiercely, "look here, you mealy-mouthed old grandma, what would you have done, if you had been there? Remember the girl was pretty as one o'clock."

I drew myself up proudly (my bathing-suit was sombre black).

"Ah, yah!" exclaimed Leander (whether he misunderstood me or not, judge you) "you're too good, Just. There's such a thing as being too rotten good. Do you know what I heard a girl say the other day, Just? 'Look here,' she said, 'you know that Sturgis man. He's like Aristides. I'm sick of hearing him called the Just'."

*A sketch
published in*
The Wave *of*
August 7, 1897.

There was only one thing to do at such a crisis. I did it. I pushed Leander into the water. His yell was drowned in a liquid gurgle, and the salmon-pink silk bathing-suit disappeared beneath the brown waters of the "Lure-you-in" Baths as Leander sank from sight.

Avis au lecteur—He came up again.

"JUSTIN STURGIS"

IV. *Showing the plausible mistake of a misguided eastern man.*

*A sketch
published in*
The Wave *of*
August 14, 1897.

Last night I went over into the Latin Quarter to play "Bocce" with an Italian friend of mine who works in a cigarette factory and is perhaps an anarchist. "Bocce" is a kind of game that involves much rolling of little balls in dirt alleys underneath "wineshops"—a sort of combination of tenpins and golf and marbles. It's fairish exercise, and vin ordinaire in tin pint measures tastes very good thereafter; also a dish of salad with just a suspicion of garlic, and a quarter of black bread rubbed with an onion. I went to the "Red House" for this wine and salad and bread, and who should I meet there—there of all places—but Leander.

"Heigh-ho," says he, with a great sigh as we settled ourselves to the barked and blackened table.

"This is a wicked world, Just'." "Many an Amen to that," says I, rubbing onion on my black bread. "When did you find it out?"

A sketch published in The Wave of *August 14, 189-.*

"Twenty-three years seven months and ten days ago."

"You surprise me. What happened twenty-three years seven months and ten days ago, to brand that hateful truth upon your conscience?"

"I was born."

I had nothing more to say.

"And recent events," sighed Leander, "have but confirmed my theory."

"Ah, for instance?"

"A man and a girl—"

"There's trouble coming."

"Big trouble; I almost punched his head."

"There would have been worse trouble if you had."

"I know that, but *noblesse oblige*, you know."

"What did the man do to awaken your nobility?"

"Said things about the girl."

"Was she a nice girl?"

"Very—and he was a nice man, only—"

"Only what?"

"He misunderstood the girl."

"San Francisco man?"

"No; Eastern."

"San Francisco girl?"

"Yes—very much so."

"That's so, you said she was a nice girl. But if he

*A sketch
published in
The Wave of
August 14, 1897.*

was an Eastern man, why was his head to be punched, especially if he was nice?"

"Well, he didn't know how to gauge a California girl—this girl, anyhow—thought she was fast."

"Gracious! Did you enlighten him?"

"Tried to but failed."

"Explain."

"It was at the club."

"Yes; well?"

"I had given the Eastern man a two weeks' card. Some half dozen of us were sitting at the window watching the world go by."

"You mean you were watching for girls."

"Well, by and by this girl came along."

"And?"

"Well, she came by; we all saw her; of course, all of us knew her, but we didn't say anything, because—"

"Because why, Leander?"

"Well, there's a certain crowd of fellows in that club —we're pretty small, though—but somehow we don't believe in mentioning a girl's name indiscriminately amongst a lot of men."

"Hear! Hear!" said I, rapping on the table, "Leander, you must put me up there."

"Why, you're one of the directors."

"Oh, that club! Well, go on. Has the girl got by?"

"Not yet; we sat there looking at her and thinking what a pretty, stylish little girl—she's very young—

A sketch published in The Wave *of August 14, 18 .*

she was, and how very jolly and companionable, when this Eastern man ups and out with:

" 'Hello, there's little so and so.' "

"I say, that was rough; what happened?"

"None of us said a word, and I began to talk about something else, but my Eastern man wouldn't down; says he: 'Jolly little piece, that.'

"Says I, mighty stiff, 'I don't think the young lady is under discussion!' 'Well, let's discuss her,' says he; 'she's the gayest, chicest, jolliest little girl I've met between the two oceans; you got lot's like that out here?' "

"Then what happened?"

"Well, then he rather saw that he'd put his foot in it, and he says, 'Well—pardon me—but—but she's fast, isn't she?' I say, Just', you ought to have seen that crowd. Every one of the fellows was just getting ready to say something very politely noble and crushing, and I was wondering if I hadn't better punch his head without saying anything, when my man says: 'I've every reason to think that I am right'; and do you know what his reasons were, Just'?"

"Think I do; shall I guess?"

"Go ahead."

"She was one of the kind of girls we spoke of once before—a little cigarette smoking, a little cocktail drinking, and perhaps the man had kissed her."

"Several times."

A sketch published in The Wave of *August* 14, 1897.

"And he had gauged her according to those things."

"He'd only known the Eastern girl, you see."

"I see. There are only two kinds of girl back there. The positively good and the positively bad, and he thought if this particular girl wasn't one she was the other."

"Exactly, and the worst of it is he will always be in doubt about her. He went away yesterday. He'd only seen the little girl a few times, and it never came to the point when she could show herself to be the good girl she really was. He never asked her to take supper with him, for instance, and so he's gone away with the impression that she's fast, and that we've got lots like that out here."

"It's rotten," said I, exasperated.

"And was he altogether to blame?" said Leander, as he rapped for the check.

"JUSTIN STURGIS"

Opinions of Justin Sturgis by Leander

A sketch published in The Wave of *August* 21, 1897.

One day last week I went out to the park, early, before anyone else was there, and rowed a bit on Stow Lake. Thereafter, being very hungry, I sought out the Japanese tea garden in the clump of trees not far from the museum. It's really delightful in this quaint, quiet, little tea garden early in the morning,

A sketch published in The Wave *of August 21, 1897*

and the beverage is of the very best. I fancied that a cup of very strong, hot tea, with crisp little Japanese cakes, would not be at all amiss. But as I came into the garden who should I find sipping his tea, smoking his morning cigar and flirting the pages of a novel but my friend, Justin Sturgis.

"Well," said he, as I dropped down beside him, "where do you come from?"

"Oh," replied I, "from going to and fro upon the earth and walking up and down in it."

"What a devil of a fellow you must be, Leander."

"I'm seeking what I may devour, if you persist in being Biblical," said I, and I ordered tea and cakes.

I was feeding my cakes to the carp and goldfish, when I noticed that Just' was looking at me gravely and shaking his head.

"Leander," says he, "it don't pay to have opinions."

"Pooh!" I answered. "Doctors and lawyers get rich on theirs."

"Yes, but their opinions are asked for; yours are not."

"Mine ought to be the more welcome, then. You must pay a lawyer for his opinions. I give mine away free, even put a chromo-lithograph in every package."

"The people you have opinions about don't like you any better though—drop 'em out, Leander. Just send 'em the chromo."

"What, now—what makes you talk like this?"

"People—girls—answer you through the medium of the press."

A sketch published in The Wave of *August 21, 1897.*

"Have you been getting any more letters?" said I, uneasily.

"Yes," said he, "and worse; we have been parodied. Listen, my child, and you shall hear," he quoted, unfolding a paper. "Listen, and see what you have brought upon yourself."

This is what Just' read:

The Opinions of Cassandra

Last night I dropped into the C. E. meeting. I am not an active member, but a girl of my spirit naturally likes to see life. I settled myself in a chair, and pulling out a package of tutti-frutti I proceeded to make myself comfortable. I was dropping into a reverie when a rustle of silk skirts caused me to look up. "What," *said I,* "you here, of all places, Cassandra?"

Cassandra grinned.

"Heigh-ho," *says she.* "I have just been to the Orpheum with Leander. You know Leander, don't you?"

"Yes," *said I, looking deep;* "miserable little snob!"

Cassandra looked hurt. "He has always been very nice to me. What have you got against him?"

"Well, I have enough against him. The other night he called on me, and you know he's awfully struck on me, and, besides, he's awfully bashful. Well, we sat on the sofa, and the first thing I knew the light went out."

"Didn't pay your gas bill," *grinned Cassandra.*

"And—well—well, he kissed me."

*A sketch
published in
The Wave of
August 21, 1897.*

"Phyllis!" gasped Cassandra.

"Course I was awfully cut up, not being used to that sort of thing, but I knew he was too bashful to speak, so I considered it as good as an engagement."

"Well," said Cass.

"The next day he wrote it up in The Surf, *saying I led him on. Did you ever hear anything so dreadful?"*

"O, I don't know. We had a fine time at the Orpheum, and I like him. If—"

But here the Endeavorers commenced the closing hymn and Cass and I left.

"Now," said Just', looking up from the paper, "what do you think of that?"

I confess I was staggered, but I began to protest feebly.

"I didn't give that girl cause to think I was bashful, did I, and I'm not 'struck on her' as she says, and she's not 'struck' on me. If we'd been 'struck on' each other it would have been all right."

"Well, then, she's not 'struck on' you as you say. What were her words, 'miserable little snob'?"

I crossed a leg uneasily. "Let's talk of something else."

"As you please," said Just', "and to begin with, or to end with (for I don't think we shall talk together much after to-day), you, Leander, who have been carrying on so about the vagaries of the San Francisco girls—"

*A sketch
published in
The Wave of
August 21, 1897.*

"And the men, too."

"And the men, too, have pointed out the evil, but can't you suggest also the remedy?"

"Heaven and earth," I gasped, "because certain things go wrong according to my notion why should I, of all people, be expected to set them right?"

"At least let us defend our opinions. If we are to give them away, let's send 'em well wrapped up and protected from breakage and weather."

"Well," replied I, "it isn't necessary to tell a girl not to smoke cigarettes nor drink cocktails, is it?"

"Might tell 'em what the men think of it."

"Humph, they'd say they didn't do it to please the men."

"Then they must do it because they have a taste for tobacco and alcohol—"

"Horrors!"

"Which is much worse."

"The men think they are little fools."

"And say so to each other."

"And about the girls that allow themselves to be kissed by men whom they are not 'struck on' and who are not 'struck on' them, and permit the 'little familiarities' we were talking about?"

"The men think they are mighty cheap."

"And say so to each other."

"But aren't there some men who kiss and don't tell?"

"That's what some girls think," said I. "But when a

*A sketch
published in
The Wave of
August 21, 189*

man can kiss a girl easily, it's the nature of the beast
to let other men know about it."

"I guess yes," said Just', scratching his head. "You
see it stands to reason that if a girl don't mind being
kissed she doesn't mind having it known. If you win
a girl easy you can't respect her very much. You'd
just as soon talk about her. And if you don't say
right out that the next man can kiss her, you say
'Hoh! yes, So-and-so, you can have a good time with
her.' "

"Sounds fine, don't it," said I. "The girls ought to
hear, but how about the young fellows who come to
functions drunk and dance with the girls?"

"The girl is to blame for that. She ought to refuse to
dance with a man when he's that way—call him down
so hard that it will almost sober him, or, better still,
tell some other man about it—some other man who is
'struck on' her."

"Would the other man punch his head?"

"He ought to. Suppose it was the girl you know—
the one particular girl. For instance, Miss——"

"We won't discuss 'that girl'," I interrupted, glaring
at him fiercely.

"That's so, and that makes me think. The men have
got something to learn, too."

"For instance."

"Well, for one thing, never to talk of a good, straight
girl among themselves; say nothing about her, good,

*A sketch
published in
The Wave of
August 21, 1897.*

bad or indifferent. You know yourself how it cheapens a girl to have her talked about in a club, or anywhere, when men get together. I've heard it done in a bar-room, even, and I know a man who used to telephone to a girl from the Deception Saloon."

"Beast!"

"No. This man didn't think, I guess. Maybe that's the trouble with most of 'em. A little more conven-tion, that's what we all need—nothing stiff or formal or false or prudish. I hate it as bad as any of them, but in Heaven's name let's have some girls who don't let every man that's known 'em a month sit with them in the dark and kiss 'em when he likes, and let's have —or, rather, let's say we've got to have, in the name of ordinary decency, men who will not come to func-tions drunk or get intoxicated where nice girls are around."

"Surely it's little enough to ask."

"Is this our last talk?"

"Guess yes."

"Then here's to a better state of things next season."

We raised our cups.

"Tea and toast," said I.

"It's mildly appropriate to drink that toast in tea," answered Just'. "Here's to conventionalities in mod-eration."

"Amen and Amen," said I.

And we drank—standing up.